Denial

Jon Raymond

SIMON & SCHUSTER

New York London Toronto Sydney New Delhi

Simon & Schuster
1230 Avenue of the Americas
New York, NY 10020

First Simon & Schuster hardcover edition July 2022

SIMON & SCHUSTER and colophon are
registered trademarks of Simon & Schuster, Inc.

For information about special discounts for bulk purchases,
please contact Simon & Schuster Special Sales at 1-866-506-1949
or business@simonandschuster.com.

The Simon & Schuster Speakers Bureau can bring authors to your
live event. For more information or to book an event,
contact the Simon & Schuster Speakers Bureau at 1-866-248-3049
or visit our website at www.simonspeakers.com.

Interior design by Kyle Kabel

Manufactured in the United States of America

1   3   5   7   9   10   8   6   4   2

Library of Congress Control Number: 2022933022

ISBN 978-1-9821-8183-3
ISBN 978-1-9821-8185-7 (ebook)

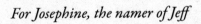

For Josephine, the namer of Jeff

1

To look into my own eyeball seemed wrong, but there it was, floating in a cylinder of pale blue light. I'd barely lifted the scanning helmet and already the final layers of the hologram's architectural netting were coming into shape, rebuilding the orb's structure from the core. The color started pouring in next, painting the sclera white and the pupil black, and then the iris ballooned with hazel and splinters of brown, mixing into that marbled, light-shot round. Hairline blood vessels branched into the vitreous humor, and the faint outline of the central canal shaded in, dividing the lobes. It was like watching the whole, wet organ mature in time-lapse.

"Here's the left one," Dr. Breeze said. He passed his hands over his controls, and another light cylinder appeared on the imaging platform, another spheroid eye growing inside. Now there were two floating eyes, staring straight at me, plucked out of my skull by the wonders of Dr. Breeze's tomographic supertech.

"Definitely some cataracts forming," he said. "You've been getting some halos at night, you said?"

"I have," I said.

"Look here," he said, drilling into the cornea with a little light wand and uncovering the gooey lens. "This area should be totally clear, but there's some clouding starting to happen. You see that? That's the cataracts. Nothing major at this point. It's normal for your age."

I tried to see the cloudiness Dr. Breeze was talking about, but the separate parts were a tangle of glistening, indistinct membranes, nothing like the diagrams in a book. I might've asked for more information, but Dr. Breeze was already wandering over to his workstation to read the fresh data streaming into his monitors. He tapped his keyboard, pulling up interpenetrating screens and graphs, casually manipulating the left eyeball by remote. The eye rotated on its axis and grew to reveal its finer detailing. It pumped up to the size of a grapefruit, an office globe, a beach ball. From his monitors, Dr. Breeze peeled back the whole cornea, slitting through layers of aqueous organ into the depths.

"Any plans for the holidays?" he said, doing his bedside conversation routine.

"Nothing much," I said. "You?"

"Some family's coming in from out of town," he said. "They like to drink and eat. We'll go to some restaurants."

"Sounds nice," I said.

"I was going to go out and cut a tree this weekend," he said, "but the kids all cried about it. They say they don't want a Christmas tree this year. It's murder."

"Kids are pretty sensitive these days, aren't they?" I said.

"They think in a different way than we did," he said, "that's for sure. I always liked going out and getting a tree when I was their age. The hot chocolate, the smell of the sap. Not how they want it anymore. I was talking to my son the other day, and he was saying the tree farmers are running death camps. We should put them all in jail."

"That's a little extreme," I said.

"Toronto," he said, leaning toward his monitor, altering his settings. "The kids want to put everyone on trial. They feel like they missed something. Maybe they've got a point, but still, I don't really—"

Dr. Breeze interrupted his speech with a little sound in his throat, not the kind you want to hear from your doctor. He didn't explain anything but returned his attention to his monitors, leaving his words and my mangled eyeball hanging.

The gentle padding of his fingertips on his plastic keyboard became the only sound in the room. I sat there looking at my destroyed eye. The left eye was still bloated and enormous, with deep gouges in the jelly and a rip opening all the way to the branching fibrils that attached to the optic nerve. The right eye was small but intact, staring off into the corner. It was disconcerting. Maybe this was what people felt like back in the nineteenth century when they saw their photographs, I thought, like some personal essence had been extracted and abused.

Dr. Breeze rose and approached the holographic eyeballs, inspecting them from different angles. He was almost exactly my age, my height, my hair color. The algorithm had really gone overboard on this pairing. I watched him watching my eyeball, awaiting his reassuring words.

"Cataracts are a naturally occurring condition," Dr. Breeze said. "The cloudiness in the lens is causing a diffusion of light in the vitreous humor here. It explains the sensitivity you were talking about. You should probably get a new prescription. You don't smoke or drink these days, do you?"

"Not anymore," I said.

"Good," he said. "And you're not obese." He spun the enlarged eye with his little wand again and zoomed in even closer. He didn't say anything as he peered at the macula and the surrounding blood vessels.

"Are you seeing something in there?" I said.

"Something," he said, distracted. "Probably nothing."

He rotated the sphere one more time and blew it up even larger, to the point of data breakdown. The eye outgrew the platform, and we could only see a detail. The clarity was abraded, the foundational pixels showing through.

"Here," he said, pointing at some smudges in the depths of the iris. We were down into the zone of microscopic information now. The smudges could be mitochondria under a microscope or blurry topographies on Mars.

"These are called prions," he said. "They're misfolded proteins. In and of themselves, they're harmless enough, but they can cause other proteins to lose their shape, and that isn't so great. They can also indicate the beginning of several neurodegenerative diseases. You don't eat beef, do you?"

"God, no," I said. The last hamburger I'd eaten had been somewhere in the vicinity of 2028.

"Squirrel?" he said.

"No."

"Any trips to Papua New Guinea? Or Kuwait?"

"Nope."

"Okay, that's good news," Dr. Breeze said. "In some cases, this kind of prion can lead to what we call spongiform encephalopathies, and that can get very ugly. Very ugly indeed."

I felt a needle of fear jab my skin, releasing a numbing agent, preparing me for what those ugly symptoms might be. Dr. Breeze continued staring at the giant, ripped, holographic eyeball, looking straight at me but focused on another plane.

"The prions are basically like termites in wood," he said. "They turn the healthy tissue into cobwebs. The word *prion* is a compound of *protein* and *infection*, so, you see, the growth is kind of like an invasion from inside your own body. Life expectancy is only a year once the symptoms kick in. And unfortunately there's no cure. The diagnosis is one hundred percent fatal."

"And what are the symptoms, exactly?" I said.

"It starts with a fever," he said. "That leads to problems speaking and swallowing, then to memory loss and dementia and coma. It's very painful the whole way through. You end up dying of pneumonia in most cases."

He said this with none of the friendliness that coated his opinions about music or books. I stared at my eye floating in front of me. The blood vessels were a wild maze inside the flayed layers. I'd walked into Dr. Breeze's office assuming I'd come out with a new eyeglass prescription. I hadn't imagined I'd come in and face my doom.

"So, what are the chances?" I said, since he wasn't saying anything.

"Given what I'm seeing here?" Dr. Breeze said. With a click of his wand he reset my eye to pristine condition. All the cuts and slashes disappeared, leaving a gleaming, immaculate sphere floating in the air. "I'd put the odds at about, say, one in a million."

*　　*　　*

I walked out of Dr. Breeze's office a half hour later, into the late-autumn, late-afternoon sun, feeling like it was a good day to keep on walking. I had a few deadlines at work, but nothing that pressing. The last flaming leaves were sticking to the trees, the rush-hour cars were flowing home in their silent aisles, and over the hills, beyond the radio towers, the sky was raining light.

Something about Death appearing on the horizon just to tip his hat and walk away put a nice glow on everything.

I headed downtown, against the current of bike commuters and scooter traffic. I heard someone singing in a tent. On the Steel Bridge, I paused for a boat protest going by, a motley little armada of canoes and motorboats decked with flags, manned by a bunch of kids in black bandannas. These days, the protests were a permanent fixture in town, like fire hydrants or garbage trucks. At all times, somewhere, a crowd was massing to remind the rest of us of some social injustice or historical wrong. This month the big subject was the Toronto Trials, twenty years old next year. It was hard to believe.

This group was flying the old logos, shouting the old slogans. "Solidarity with Air!" "Solidarity with Trees!" "Solidarity with Rock!" Most of them looked like they hadn't been born at the time of the verdicts, but that only seemed to make their rage stronger. They were like Breeze's kid, still wanting to make someone pay. In a few hours, they'd all end up downtown for the ritual glass breaking, maybe a mattress bonfire, more call-and-response. In the morning, the shopkeepers would sweep up the damage and file their insurance claims, and what was the point? Every revolution became a bureaucracy in the end. Someday they'd understand that. Although maybe some never would.

Passing under the bridge, the protestors' voices became echoey before brightening again as they came out the other side. Soon the boats had disappeared around the bend, leaving a dimpled, silver wake, and I continued my way downtown, through the early gangs of weekend partiers, the knots of young dudes, the gaggles of bachelorettes. I passed through clouds of weed smoke and clouds of peppermint vape smoke, making my way up the hill toward the eyewear emporium in the shopping district in Northwest where all my fresh optometric data had already flowed.

"Hi, Jack," the young woman in the foyer said. "Welcome. Billing information the same?"

"Should be," I said.

"Great," she said. "Come on in. Modern frames are on level three. We're glad you're here."

The elevator door opened into a giant white room scattered with about a dozen customers in their VR goggles, doing the silly tai chi of the virtual retail experience. My own goggles appeared almost immediately, delivered by a kid in a white jumpsuit, and when I slipped them on, the room subtly changed hue. A pinkish color rose on the walls, and the air filled with rows of frames floating at shoulder height. Tortoiseshell. Rimless. Pentagonal. They snapped into focus, grouped by style, as beside me appeared a hovering, virtual hand mirror.

I waded into the rows and started my browsing. The first pair I tried were oval tortoiseshells with a powerful zoom function. The controls were different from my old glasses, and I accidentally zoomed in on a woman in the cat-eye section, ogling the scuffs of her clogs, the creases of her elbow, and when I zoomed back out, I found she was staring straight at me. It was kind of embarrassing for a second, but I managed to pretend nothing had happened. I took a long moment to alter my mirror settings, upping the contrast, fixing the gain, and then, casually, let the tortoiseshells fade and kept browsing.

I tested some thick purple frames, some round white frames, some wire rims. Each pair had its own interesting character, but none seemed right for my face. I was at the age where I wanted glasses that read as dangerous yet mature, rebellious yet scholarly, glasses that said I was seasoned but not totally done with life yet. Was that too much to ask? I knew I'd probably end up with the same horn-rims I'd been wearing since my late teenage days, but I kept looking anyway, just for fun. I was almost fifty, and feeling lucky. Maybe now was the time for a complete style update.

As I moved through the aisles, swiping at frames, I noticed the woman in cat eyes hadn't stopped looking at me. Her gaze seemed to follow me around, exerting a constant pressure on the side of my face. I wondered if she'd sensed the zoom somehow after all, but that seemed impossible. Or maybe she was just checking me out. Could it be? It'd been a long time since I'd entered into that little game, but the mechanics weren't hard to recollect. The little glances going back and forth. The invisible strings springing to life. Nothing would come of it in the end, I knew, but it was always a pleasant chemistry while it lasted.

I paused in the wireless aisle and allowed her a clean look at my profile, and then, gradually, I worked my way into her blind spot. It turned out she was about my age, as far as I could tell.

Medium height. Hard bangs. Nice arm shape. Her cheek was smooth and olive-complected, obscured by her ragged rocker bob, and her clothes were youthful but well-put-together. She wore a yellow, short-sleeved sweatshirt, a denim miniskirt, and lavender clogs. She had a very nice-looking backside.

I watched her try on a pair of hot pink frames and for a second caught a sliver of her face in her mirror. She had pretty lips, a graceful chin, a kind of squashed-looking nose. I was only catching fragments of her, but something about her features struck me as familiar. I tried finding the connection in my memory but whatever impressions I had floated at the edges of my mind, out of reach. Maybe I'd worked with her somewhere, I thought, or bought something from her at a grocery store. And then, suddenly, a name came to me. *Sobie.*

Sobie was her last name, I remembered, but that was what we used to call her. She'd dated my friend Jude for a while, and she'd lived with a person named Charles in a house with a broken hot tub. In our twenties, we'd gone to many parties together and sat in many of the same bars, though I couldn't recall us ever being in a room together by ourselves.

Sobie had clearly recognized me but didn't seem that eager to make contact. I could understand. We hadn't seen each other in twenty-five years, and in that time many big changes had occurred. Entire worlds had come and gone. If a person didn't want to look back, no excuse was necessary as far as I was concerned. But even as we continued our browsing, giving each

other our space, building a kind of force field of mutual oblivi-
ousness, I could tell she was keeping track of me. It was possible
I even caught a flicker of mild disbelief in her eyes, like she still
couldn't entirely convince herself it was me.

In the end, we started talking almost by accident. Or maybe
we engineered it, it was hard to tell, it was such a delicate,
unstated agreement we'd fallen into. We both picked our frames
at about the same time and went to the main desk to place our
orders. The store imaged the frames on-site, and during the lag
time the customers were sent to a waiting area. The waiting area
was another white room, much smaller than the showroom,
with blond wooden benches and a few tables with simple flower
arrangements in Mason jars, expressly real. I went in and most
of the seats were already taken, so I decided to go ahead and sit
on the bench near Sobie and see what transpired.

"Sobie," I said.

"Jack," she said. She'd always had a funny, understated way
about her, I remembered now, and her black eyes had always had
that slightly amused, belligerent sparkle. Her voice was exactly
the same—low, slightly guarded, a little weary.

"How's it going?" I said.

"Pretty good," she said. "You know. Up and down. You?"

"Getting by."

Discreetly, we were both scanning for age marks, looking
at ring fingers. The meeting was made all the stranger by the
heightened, return-to-reality effect from the goggles we'd just

been wearing. And then, on my side, by the fading death magic of my prions.

"Are you visiting town or something?" she said. "I haven't seen you around in forever."

"I moved away," I said. "And then I moved back. About a year ago."

"Hardly anyone moves back," she said.

"I got a job," I said. "It was hard to say no."

"What kind of job?" she said.

"At a newspaper," I said.

"You're a reporter?" she said.

"Yeah," I said.

"That's right," she said. "I remember you liked to write."

We'd arrived at the first fork in our conversation. We could either keep things shallow and talk about the weather or politics, or we could go somewhere deeper and try to get into something personal. I had the sense we were both willing to go deeper, but that left us a lot of options. Health? Family? Kids? Thankfully, we had one giant topic between us, which was all the people we'd known. It turned out we only had to say a name and a whole world of association flowed into our heads, a whole glittering tree of ganglia that very few people in the world besides us shared.

"You ever talk to Trey?" I said.

"He's in Sacramento," Sobie said. "He's working for the city. In parks. He doesn't love it."

"How about Heather?" I said.

"Which Heather?" she said.

"The one who set her hair on fire that time," I said, "with the blowtorch."

"You mean the Heather who lived in that apartment over the bowling alley," she said.

"Yeah, that one," I said.

"She's a nurse now," she said. "The other Heather died, actually. Liver failure. It was really sad."

We kept going like that, saying names back and forth as the other customers came and went. Sobie had good intelligence on many of our old friends, which I found impressive because a lot of them had disappeared along the way. We'd all been reckless people then. We'd betrayed each other and failed each other in many ways. But for those who'd come out on the other side, who'd graduated in a sense, a certain understanding was shared. It was hard to explain what that understanding was, exactly, but Sobie and I both seemed to have it.

"You remember that guy Gabe?" she said.

"He didn't like to wear a shirt very much, did he?" I said.

"I wonder if he has to wear a shirt now," she said. "Probably."

We were still catching up when the clerk appeared and handed Sobie her new glasses. She opened the box and pulled out a pair of big, magenta Yoko Onos. She put them on and blinked a few times and posed for me, turning her face side to side. She had a little scar on her lip, a white mark in the upper corner, like a faded cleft. I remembered that now, too.

"These look all right?" she said.

"They look great," I said.

"Okay," she said. "I guess I'll trust you on that."

My frames came soon after, the same old horn-rims. We didn't bother pretending they were anything special. We left the store together and walked outside to find that night had fallen. The street was busy with homecoming commuters, restaurant goers, and beggars mumbling on every corner.

We stood on the sidewalk for another few minutes, trading a few more names as the superbuses passed violently by and the crowd flowed around us. A guy played chaotic flute music from a doorstep. The whole time, a faint smile hovered on Sobie's lips, like she still had something she wanted to tell me, a little secret she wanted to get out.

"What?" I said.

"Oh, nothing," she said, shaking her head, smiling.

"Come on," I said.

"It's just, the last time I saw you," she said, "it was pretty intense, that's all."

"I don't remember," I said.

"Really?" she said. "You don't? At all?"

"I don't remember a lot from those years," I said.

"Neither do I," she said. "I wish I remembered more. But I remember this. It was in a parking lot out in East County. We were all out there for some reason. You were wearing a suit that night, I remember. It was light blue. And you had a ruffled shirt.

You were all dressed up. There was a group of teenagers who were making fun of you, and you talked back."

"That sounds like what I'd do."

"Yeah, and they really kicked your ass," she said. "It was terrible. That was the last time I saw you. You were covered in blood. I mean, it was gushing. Gushing out of your nose. Blood all over your face. All over that cheap suit, on the lapels. And you were lunging at these kids, wiping your blood on their shirts. That was your way of fighting back, I guess, with your blood. It was crazy."

"They broke my nose that night," I said. "If it's the night I'm thinking of."

"You really don't remember?" she said. "God."

"I couldn't even see the bottom at that point," I said. "I still had a long way to go."

"I thought you were dead," she said. She looked at me warmly, her new glasses flashing with the passing lights. "Anyway. It was good running into you, Jack. I'm really glad it turns out you're not dead."

2

I lived in a fourplex not very different from the place I lived in my first time through town. It was a burly Craftsman from 1912 that'd somehow avoided demolition over the years, mostly because the landlord was too lazy to make all the necessary arrangements. He was an ancient, ponytailed art photographer, and to his great credit he didn't feel the need to monetize every single asset in his life. The building wouldn't last forever, but until he was gone, we all knew we were probably safe.

I woke up on Monday still feeling upbeat. I stumbled into my little kitchen and ground the coffee beans, releasing the earthy aroma, and fried myself an egg, which came out lacy and perfectly browned. The toast popped on cue. I had fresh brewer's yeast to sprinkle on top. I was moving easily in my daily groove.

Through my first cup of coffee I checked the news, tracking the horrors unfolding around the globe. Megafires in South America, cyclones in Oklahoma, refugee riots in India. It'd been almost twenty-five years since the Upheavals began, depending on where a person put the origin—the Green Abolitionist Convergence in São Paulo, some said, others, the solar vanadium gem breakthrough—but at this point pretty much everyone could agree they weren't turning out as imagined.

I made another batch of coffee and caught the bus to work. I loved riding the bus. I sat in the back with my traveler mug and greeted the other regulars as they boarded, some with a nod, most with a respectful aversion of the eyes. The high school kids couldn't sit still, pushing and shoving each other into the aisles before tumbling off en masse at Twelfth Avenue, replaced by the nuns on their way to the shelters.

We crossed the river, and I debarked at Fifth and took the light-rail to deep Northwest and the offices of the *Constant Globe*, my employer. The *Globe* took up the ninth floor of a glass high-rise, among a cluster of glass high-rises in what used to be big-sky light industrial warehouse territory. It was a digital communications organ, or what used to be called a newspaper, and I was one of twenty-some reporters on staff, though to call it reporting was another anachronism. I collected raw feeds from a massive network of individuals scattered around the world and tried to find some kind of order in the jumble. I aggregated; I analyzed. When a riot broke out in Moscow or a mass movement swarmed a street in Cape Town, I vacuumed up the street-level chatter and turned the fragments into a singular, coherent story line. It was journalism without any physical movement on my part, but with many of the bricks of the basic pyramid intact. I had my sources. I wrote my ledes. Some days I even drew a pattern or highlighted a point of view that merited widespread public attention.

"Morning, Aliyah," I said. The managing editor was sitting at her desk as usual. She called herself managing editor, but she was really more like the publisher's personal factotum. From her seat near the door, she oversaw his many properties, paid his alimonies, scheduled his dental appointments, and arranged his dog walks. I greeted the copy editor, the line editor, and the other office coworkers I passed on my way, all well-intentioned, industrious people involved in their little turf wars and personality conflicts. The whole operation was funded by our benevolent publisher, Liu Lee, the scion of an early '90s software fortune. He'd founded the *Globe* as a bulwark of truth and accountability and independence and citizenship and verification and accuracy and conscience and a dozen other gold-plated words, although in reality he'd purchased himself a personal fiefdom. We were a team of investigators hired to pursue his fancies, and we all lived according to his whims.

Lately I'd been keeping tabs on public school districts across the nation. Liu's granddaughter was starting kindergarten, and thus the public-school beat had become a big deal at the *Globe*. From my seat near the window, I spent many hours every week trawling school newspapers, PTA newsletters, community bulletin boards, and district interoffice memos, seeking key words like *asbestos, formaldehyde, phthalates,* and *short-chain chlorinated paraffins.* I was seeking patterns in the noise and, behind the patterns, culprits to expose and bring to justice—in a word, reporting. In the spring, I'd broken a story about a nationwide surveillance system installed in elementary schools, ostensibly to exclude sexual predators but mostly used for nabbing undocumented parents. I'd won an award for that one. People had been fired. I was fine on the grade-school beat.

Between searches this morning, I rewarded myself with searches of Sobie, which was a little creepy, I realized, but hard to resist. It took about five seconds to find out she was a real estate agent with no criminal record. She owed $27 in library fines. She lived in a cute bungalow in the Cully neighborhood, out by the airport. She belonged to the community center gym. Her credit rating was less than stellar. Her music tastes leaned toward torch singers. She loved all dogs, especially a Siberian husky.

Before I knew it, I was stomping around in her private archive, observing her life from some extremely intimate angles. Her child was a girl. Her name was Eileen. She was eleven and often dressed in overalls.

I watched Eileen age backward from the day before yesterday. I paused on her ninth birthday party, with the clowns and streamers, and her swimming lessons in a sun-blasted public pool. I saw Sobie breastfeeding, and then Sobie pregnant, wearing a ski hat. A jump and I was into old party pictures, pre-Eileen, on a trip to Spain, Sobie in a bikini. A man appeared for a couple of years, but he dribbled out along the way. I saw pictures of Sobie camping, drinking in bars, eating a salad covered in flower blossoms. I felt like I was staring in all the windows of her house at once, following her down a dozen crowded streets.

I ejected from her timeline at 2037, the year of the firestorms in San Diego, the year Venice was lost. I got back to work.

*　　*　　*

I had a lunch date that day with one of my local sources, a hard-left schoolteacher named Jeff Catalog. I'd recruited him from a chat room on progressive curriculum reform in the hopes that some of his tirades might one day lead to a story or two, but so far, after six months of lunches, nothing had panned out. His broadsides against the state education commission were mostly just thinly disguised complaints about personal slights, I'd found, and his loyalty to the union was practically absolute. And yet, for some reason, I kept meeting him. He was funny, for one thing. And everything he said struck me as almost exactly half-wrong, which was kind of interesting, and sometimes caused me to think about things in a new light.

We always met at a steamy ramen shop on Second Avenue. This time, Jeff showed up covered in blisters. His forehead was peeling, and his cheeks were bright red. He'd just been to Mexico, he said, and he'd been pounded by the sun down there.

"Sun is really hot in Mexico," he said. "And you know those chemical sunblocks are full of carcinogens. So I said hell with it this time, I'll just buy a sombrero."

"Looks like it didn't work so well," I said.

"No, it worked," he said. "The sombrero was awesome. But it got really windy on the last day and it blew off my head during a hike. I think the ozone layer is closer in Mexico or something. A couple hours and I was totally scorched."

Despite the burn, Jeff seemed unusually peppy. We took our usual table next to a fogged window overlooking the street, and as soon as the waiter stepped away with our orders—spicy red miso for him, vegan tonkotsu shio for me—Jeff told me that he had something big to share.

"This is huge," he said, looking around as if there might be spies in the next booth. "I didn't want to say anything about it over the phone, in case . . . you know. But I wanted to tell you as soon as possible. I don't know if this is a good place to talk, either, now that we're here. A lot of people in the room."

"I think we're safe," I said. "I swept the whole place for bugs."

"Okay, well, don't blame me if someone scoops you," he said. "You can't be too paranoid, in my opinion. So I've told you we go down to Guadalajara every year, right? It's kind of our main place we like to go."

"You've mentioned it," I said.

"And we always stay at the same place," he said, "this little hotel on República Avenue. Lots of good parks around there, lots of good restaurants. The whole city's very cheap compared to Mexico City, which is why we go pretty much every year."

"So you've also said," I said.

"So this year we went down there again," he said. "I had some work to do, which meant I was getting up early every morning and leaving the hotel. Dianne likes her sleep on vacation. She didn't want me working in the room. It's nice but small, and the typing, she hates that. She says she can feel my brain waves. So I decided I'd go find some other place, and I ended up at the café in the regional museum down the street. Their café opened early, it's a beautiful room, just a couple blocks from our hotel. It was perfect . . ."

He kept going like this for a long time, taking tiny steps toward his point and wandering off on another tangent. I tried to pay attention, but at a certain point I started to drift. It wasn't only the digressions that distracted me, but the sunburn, too. Jeff was a trollish-looking guy on the best day. With the white pustules bubbling on his nose, the rime of leakage under his eyes, he looked genuinely disturbing. I was afraid a big shingle might peel off his bald head at any second.

When our bowls arrived, Jeff was still doing his setup. He was describing the café in great detail, the art nouveau posters on the wall, the potted tropical plants. As he stuffed wet noodles in his mouth, talking about the gentle light from the southern windows, he seemed to be coming around to some notable event.

"... and that was when he walked in," Jeff said, swabbing his mouth. "You're not going to believe this. Are you ready? The person I saw down there was Robert Cave. The Empty Chair. I swear to God. No farther away from me than I am from you."

"Mm-hmm," I said. I was deep into my own bowl now, chasing down a bright green shred of seaweed. I could tell Jeff was looking at me from across the table, awaiting my incredulous response, but something about his need just made me want to wait.

"You remember who Cave is, don't you?" he said. "One of the Thirty-Three?"

Of course I knew who Cave was. At one time, back when I was marching in the streets, I could've named every member of the Thirty-Three and recited their whole dossiers chapter and verse. There was Thomas Gold, CEO at Exxon; Brandt Hughes, CFO at Shell; the entire Chinese docket from Sinochem. For over two years, the whole world had watched as they were prosecuted in their bleachers. We'd come to know not only the defendants, but the lawyers, too, and all the bit players. Sandhya Spivak, the skinny Indian bailiff squinting at the proceedings from the side. Xavier Pompidou, the French translator who couldn't seem to give himself a clean shave. Amy Landis, the Canadian lead prosecutor with the penchant for big shoulder pads. We'd watched for hundreds of hours as Amy and her team had methodically constructed the legal concept of "crimes against life," along the way casually shredding any defense based on notions of the defendants' ignorance, utterly absurd in the year 2032, and shutting down any pleas based on the defendants' inward opposition to their own industries' activities, that never-acted-upon "conscience" that characterized so many of their bids for leniency.

Throughout 2032, we'd watched the most powerful carbon executives and lobbyists in the world stand trial, even as the fires in New Zealand raged and the smoke inversions in South America entered year four, but also as cars and planes remained idle, bio-concretes rose into vertical farms in the cities, solar panels petaled the grid, and industrial carbon-capture systems came online to filter the planet's CO_2. In that brief span of confusion and possibility, of Upheaval, Toronto had been one of the many fronts in the war of reimagining the future. Twenty years later, we still didn't know if we'd won that war or not.

If Jeff had actually seen Robert Cave, that would be big news. Among the Empty Chairs—the eight who'd been tried in absentia—the only two who'd been found were Andrei Prochevski and Akeem Amari, nabbed in their neighboring plantations in Nigeria in 2038. Since then, the others had receded into the ether, blurred by the many seasons of fire and ice. In the meantime, we'd seen the rise of the doubters, the burners, the recidivists, and the fakers. We'd seen the return of the beef industry, the splintering of international photovoltaic standards, the endless bureaucratic slog of the Environmental Racism Reconciliation Commission. There were so many new villains to keep track of, so many compromises to swallow, it was hard to remember, year to year, who all the main offenders were. Even harder to think about all the loss.

I finished my bowl as Jeff lectured me on Cave's long-ago crimes. Cave was a big one, he kept telling me. Project manager for NovaChem's pipeline from the Arctic down to Lakota Country; author of the infamous memo predicting global economic collapse if the petrol empire's supply chain went neglected; the one who'd constructed all the charts with the bogus projections that he'd delivered in hundreds of lectures on "the moral case for fossil fuels" at colleges and pseudo-academic symposia.

"And you think you saw him on your vacation," I said, tipping my bowl for the last slosh of broth.

"I saw him three times," Jeff said. "He came into the café three days in a row. He looks the same as he did before the Trials. No question."

"He would've gotten surgery or something," I said. "He wouldn't look the same."

"No," Jeff said. "He looks the same. I filmed him. Check this out..."

Jeff pulled his phone from his pocket and brought up a video and slid the phone across the table. The video was a typical Jeff production, which was to say much less than advertised. He'd shot it from behind, so I couldn't see any distinguishing features beyond his temple and his right ear. The person he'd recorded was talking to a woman at a café counter, but the espresso machine was going and I couldn't hear what anyone said. I watched it to be polite and pushed the phone back across the table, unmoved.

"It's him," Jeff said. "Believe me."

"Maybe," I said.

Jeff was adamant. He made me watch the video again, along with a video of Robert Cave giving a graduation speech in 2026. Cave was a fairly handsome fellow, tall and elegantly formed. He spoke with a measured voice and made supple hand gestures to emphasize his complicated points. There was a resemblance to the guy in the café video, I could admit, but not enough to make a positive identification. I didn't bother telling Jeff that at one-quarter profile, with all that sound pollution, his video was basically useless. You couldn't run an image like that through a commercial recognition program. You'd end up with a thousand branching possibilities. There was too much data out there. Long ago, the map of the world had outgrown the world.

"Even if it's him," I said, pushing the phone across the table again, "he was probably just visiting, like you. Going to a museum. He's gone."

"No, no, he lives there," Jeff said, getting testy, as he sometimes did when he felt unheard. "I followed him home. I didn't get his exact address but I got the street he's on. Calle Ontario. Four hundred block. He went there every day, and it isn't zoned for rental, I checked."

"Maybe you should call the cops," I said.

"Oh, hell no," he said. "I don't want to get officially involved here, man. No way. I don't need that hassle in my life. Are you kidding?"

"But you'll give me the hassle."

"I thought you'd want this hassle," he said. "Isn't it your job?"

It was amusing to see what a ferocious soldier Jeff could be so long as he kept himself a few hundred yards from any actual risk. I finally agreed to take his video, and even then he practically forced me to promise he'd never be revealed as the source. Of course not, I told him. That was one of the basic cornerstones of journalism. The source was protected. Until it wasn't, he pointed out. And I had to agree. The gravestones of whistleblowers told a sad story.

I went back to the office and watched the video a few more times at my desk, confirming it as fundamentally nothing. It was just an ear. But as I watched the footage over and over again, taking in the polite, casual quality of the exchange—this potential Empty Chair loitering in a café, flirting with the young barista—the significance started to irk me. He was drinking coffee. How was that possible? If this was in fact Robert Cave, it was a travesty. He was seventy-seven years old but looking quite spry. Even now, his old company, NovaChem, was back to its mischief, mining Greenland for zinc and anorthosite, supplying the ingredients for everything from chemical cleaners to electrical porcelain. If it was him, the world should know. A trip to sunny Guadalajara didn't sound so bad, either.

The person I had to convince to send me was Liu, our publisher. I found him in his corner office, as usual, with Aliyah, in the middle of one of their combination editorial brainstorm sessions and interior design consultations, a rolling conversation organized specifically to let Liu's mind flit from topic to topic and never come to a decision about anything.

"Come on in, Jack," Aliyah said. "We're just choosing between the black marine marble and the fantasy green marble for the countertops in Liu's brownstone in New York. What do you think? I think the fantasy marble is pretty cool."

"They both look great," I said, approaching Liu's desk where a messy array of colored tiles lay among his piles of papers and scattered books. Aliyah lounged in the window nook, overseeing.

"That doesn't help us at all," she said. "Just say fantasy marble and we're all done here. Liu respects your aesthetic opinion. Don't you, Liu?"

"How long is this going to this take?" Liu said, staring at the tiles. "I need my sink working next month. I can't tell what anything will look like with these stupid little tiles. This is ridiculous."

"I could get a 3-D mock-up made if you want," Aliyah said. "Would that help you see it better?"

"No, no!" he said. "We're not spending any more money on this!"

I could tell it wasn't the best moment to make my pitch. But then again, it was never the best moment at the *Globe*, so

I plowed onward. As Liu's attention pinged between the marble samples and the various messages streaming into his monitor, I gave a quick summary of my lunch with Jeff Catalog. Aliyah listened from her perch, nodding at all the appropriate moments, multitasking gracefully, while Liu scowled and made half-confused grunts. At one point he seemed to scribble a note to himself, which I took as a good sign, but when I finally handed him the video, hoping I was sealing my case, I realized I hadn't been getting through at all.

"You can't even see what this is," Liu said. "It's just an ear."

"True," I said, "but with the audio, we might be able to get a decent ID. And if it's a match, this is more than a normal Denier we're talking about here. It's an Empty Chair."

"There are fifty Empty Chair sightings every year," he said. "And they're all total bullshit."

"This is a firsthand sighting," I said. "The videographer just gave me the footage a few hours ago. He's a guy I've been talking to for months about—"

"That janitor in La Paz," Liu said. "Or that bus driver in Nepal? None of these guys are ever confirmed."

"I remember Robert Cave," Aliyah said, throwing me a bone. "I mean, his name on the chair. I was only a kid during Toronto. But he's a big one. I think you should think about it, Liu."

But Liu was already done. His paranoia about the tiles had transferred to the story, and convincing him of anything once he'd settled on a new bias was impossible. He'd just jostle around, refusing all arguments. Aliyah kept nudging him, trying to get him to consider a basic fact-gathering mission, but she didn't get any response, either. He said I was doing a fine job on the school-pollutants beat. He saw no reason to reassign my energies. I walked out of the office ten minutes later, rebuffed.

I'd barely gotten back to my desk when Aliyah appeared, carrying her cloth bag of tile samples.

"Seems like a good story to me," she said.

"He's right," I said, staring at my monitor, typing in my pollution key words. "These things don't ever pan out."

"It wouldn't cost very much to go check," she said. "A plane ticket, a hotel room."

"It's even cheaper if I sit here and harvest data from my desk," I said.

"If that's really Cave, it would be a huge deal," she said.

I didn't bother to respond. She stood near my shoulder as I punched in my searches. *Nitrogen Oxide. Sulfur Oxide. Sulfur Dioxide.* She shifted her bag of tiles from hand to hand. I assumed she was having some kind of internal dialogue about the nature of justice and punishment and setting examples for future generations, preparing to give me some kind of inspirational speech, but it turned out she was contemplating more practical matters.

"We could use a big story like this right now," she said. "Liu's getting bored lately, I can tell."

"Oh yeah?" I said. "How bored?"

"Dangerously bored," she said.

I kept my eyes on the screen. *Benzene. Formaldehyde.* The amount of money Liu hemorrhaged on the *Globe* every month was a closely guarded secret, but we all knew it was surely enormous. He didn't seem to mind spending it as long as our readership remained steady and a trickle of acclaim from the prize-granting committees kept coming in. We all knew the moment he stopped enjoying himself, however, the whole operation could easily fold, like so many of his other vanity projects through the years. Aliyah was implying that moment was closer than I thought.

She stood there, shifting the bag from palm to palm. Her tiles made a glassy, muffled clatter inside the fabric. I continued my scrolling. *Methylmercury. Cadmium.* Good old *lead.*

"I'll talk to him," Aliyah said. "No promises." And she exited, swinging her tinkling bag at her waist.

3

Sobie wasn't that surprised when I got in touch with her later in the week. I imagined she probably dealt with guys like me all the time—guys on the street, ghouls from the past, popping out of doorways, looking to worm their way into her life. To her credit, she didn't make me feel like a fool for sending her a note. She wrote back in a matter of minutes and seemed agreeable to spending some time together. She warned me that finding that time wouldn't be so simple, however. She was a single mom, she wrote. She had a job. If I wanted to see her anywhere in the next month, I'd have to go with her to do a boring errand on Saturday.

"My daughter's having a sleepover," she wrote, "and I have to go pick out a fruit tree at a nursery. It's like an hour out of town. Sorry, but it's my only real window."

"That sounds all right," I wrote. "I like trees."

"Totally okay if you don't want to go," she wrote.

"No," I wrote. "I like a drive."

"You're sure?" she wrote.

"Yeah," I wrote.

"Okay," she wrote. "Then I guess I'll pick you up at four."

*   *   *

Saturday was cold and damp. A scattering of dead, wet leaves wheezed on the sidewalk as Sobie glided to a stop in one of those mini, carbon-battery-powered flex cars in front of my apartment. The door opened, and I swung into the capsule, folding myself into a ball, and off we motored into the afternoon traffic.

Driving through town, Sobie split her attention between the traffic and the strange, new person in the car with her. She seemed unsure what this was supposed to be. I didn't know, exactly, either. It wasn't a date, though maybe it was something resembling a date, or something preliminary to a date. Not that we were the kind of people who went on dates, anyway.

"So, how's your apartment?" she said. "I've always wondered about that building. I've driven by probably a thousand times."

"It's nice," I said. "I like it pretty well."

"And how about your neighborhood?" she said.

"It's good," I said. "Good coffee. Good bread. A decent bookstore. Yeah."

"I show a lot of houses in your neighborhood," she said. "Great walking scores."

She found a little better traction with questions about my work. She'd clearly done some research since we'd run into each other, and she had some lines of inquiry prepared.

"So you were in DC in the thirties?" she said. "That must've been intense."

"It was," I said. "I was just getting started. I had no idea what I was doing out there."

"And then you joined a media collective or something?" she said.

"I guess technically I cofounded it," I said.

"And you interviewed the vice president?" she said.

"She wasn't the vice president yet," I said. "But yeah, a couple times."

It became obvious quickly that Sobie didn't have much interest in current events. The big names and dates were a vague jumble to her. At one time I might've judged her for that, but at this point it didn't bother me at all. If ignoring the poison of the daily news cycle helped a person get through their life, that was fine by me. As Sobie kept asking questions, though, probing further, I got the sense she had a genuine interest in the actual labor of reporting—the craft of it, the process—and as we gathered speed on the outskirts of town, I found myself going into some detail about the search algorithms I used and my strategies around examining defunct digital archives. It was strange, hearing myself talking like an expert about something. Strange to realize I'd actually devoted my life to something. Strangest of all to realize I even had some principles.

"So if you need footage from a surveillance camera, for instance," she said, "how do you go about getting it?"

"The owner of the building is the one you talk to," I said. "The property owner owns the footage. So you track down the owner."

"And how do you find out who owns a building?" she said.

"The city has a record of that," I said. "At least in the United States that's how it works. It's different overseas. But it can be complicated here, too, if the building belongs to a hedge fund or a publicly traded company or something."

"Interesting."

Soon we were zooming through the southern suburbs, light-rail trains flashing by in either direction, and I got the feeling it was time to ask her some questions. I tried to keep the conversation symmetrical by asking her about her work.

"It's kind of like your job," she said. "I've got my sources. I follow my leads. I figure out chains of ownership. A lot of it is the same, really. A lot of it is storytelling, honestly."

"And did you always want to be in real estate?" I said.

"Well, I always liked going into houses," she said. "I always liked seeing how people lived. I always wanted to peek in windows. So I guess so, yeah." She laughed. "It was my calling."

Soon we'd punctured the growth boundary. We started rolling through a fertile savannah of wheat fields dotted with oak trees and old barns. The sun made its late-day appearance, bathing the landscape in golden light, falling over fallow fields edged with glittering windbreaks. We passed signs for tamales, honey, and corn mazes, and every once in a while the peak of the mountain floated into view. We talked about the other jobs we'd had, the minor humiliations we'd endured, and some of the mistakes we'd made at the expense of our coworkers. She had a lot of good stories about a thrift store/bagel shop she'd once managed.

And then, suddenly, around a bend, the nursery appeared—an oasis between low-rising, stubbled hills. Sobie steered us into the gravel lot, and we climbed from the pod into the clean country air. We stretched our legs and breathed deeply. Our city was quiet, but out here, the quiet was of a whole different order. We could hear the wind in the wild grass, the far-distant hum of a tractor. I heard the ruffle of a bird's wings passing overhead.

"Okay," she said. "Fruit trees. Where would they be?"

"Usually the big stuff is in the back," I said.

"Do you know something about fruit trees?" she said.

"Not really," I said.

"Damn," she said. "Neither do I."

The main storefront of the nursery was a Quonset hut barricaded by potted palm and date trees. We passed through a gateway and came out on the rear patio where a few people were browsing annuals, perennials, bulbs, and ferns. We continued down an aisle of bonsais, past some currants and azaleas, heading for the taller saplings we could see beyond the greenhouses.

"So what kind of tree are you looking for?" I said.

"I don't know," she said. "I want something that flowers. Something that gives some shade. Something that won't take forever to start fruiting."

"How big are you thinking?" I said.

"Like, fifteen feet?" she said. "Stone fruit is what I want. Something juicy."

We went to the rows of stone fruit trees. The saplings were about eight feet tall. Among the choices in stock were nectarines, plums, peaches, cherries, and apricots, but at this stage they all looked more or less identical. The trunks were like tall, flimsy broomsticks with thin branches forking toward the light. The leaves were barely visible, small oval stubs, shiny, dark green on one side, light green on the other. Sobie started walking the rows, inspecting the leaves and bark, using her imagination as to what the trees might become.

"Does your daughter like nectarines?" I said. I was reading the tag on a nectarine sapling.

"She doesn't eat fruit," Sobie said.

"Oh, too bad," I said.

"She might sell it, though," she said. "She sells anything. She takes her old stuffed animals and drawings out onto the street and sells them to people walking by. It's incredible. People stop on their motorcycles, in their vans. They buy all of her crap. She makes a hundred dollars in an afternoon sometimes. She'll probably be a fruit monger. For a few days, at least."

"She sounds like a smart kid," I said.

"She is smart," she said. "We'll see how the business model holds up when she isn't so cute anymore."

Sobie kept inspecting the trees, telling me more about her daughter as she went. Her daughter was small for her age, she said. She often acted like a dog. She prided herself on her flexibility. She had a couple of distinct friend groups, the nerds and the jocks. The genotypes were still going strong, Sobie informed me, generation after generation, they never changed.

"Is her dad somewhere in the picture?" I said casually.

"He's gone, thank God," Sobie said. "He was the worst guy I was ever with. It's such a shame, you know? I've been with so many nice guys over the years. Tons of great guys. And then, of course, it's the ugliest, meanest one who gets me pregnant. I mean, other guys got me pregnant, just never at the right time. He was there at the right time, I'll give him that. But what a terrible person. I really hope he never shows up again in my life."

"What's he doing now?" I said.

"Living in Montana or something," she said.

"And no one else has come along?" I said.

"There hasn't been time, Jack," Sobie said. "I'm putting up a good front for you, but being a single, working parent is hard work. Really fucking hard. I'm just starting to get to where I can even think about something like that."

All the while, Sobie continued scraping the bark, looking at the color of the trunk underneath, and touching leaves, checking for insect gnaw or rot. She knew a little more than she let on. She was also faced with a more complicated decision than I'd realized. She was weighing the growth of these trees against her daughter's years at home, placing the overlapping windows of time on top of each other, seeing how they matched up.

How old would Eileen be when this tree bloomed? she was calculating. When it fruited? How large would this tree be when Eileen left home? When, and if, she returned?

Gradually, Sobie winnowed down her decision to two choices: plum and cherry. They were both classics, we agreed. You couldn't go wrong, either way.

"What do you think?" she said, standing back and comparing two potted trees. Beads of water clung to the leaves of both, tiny orbs filled with tiny refractions. The trunks of both were reddish and svelte.

"Cherry blossoms look great in the spring," I said.

"For about a week," Sobie said. "True."

"And plums taste good," I said. "Especially the Italian ones."

"You're not going to help me decide this, are you?" she said. "You're just going to tell me what you think I want to hear."

"I really don't think there's a wrong answer," I said.

"I like the spring cherry blossoms," Sobie said, touching the leaves of the cherry tree once again, deliberating. "But I can see those all over the place. I think I like plums better for eating. They're better in crisps and cobblers. I'd like to make more of those."

"Judge a tree by its fruit," I said.

"Yeah, okay," she said. "I'll do the plum."

*   *   *

She paid for the tree and scheduled delivery in the front office. She also picked up a packet of tomato seeds and new hand clippers. We exited and walked back to the car. It was not even six o'clock.

The tree decision finished, we now had another decision before us. The drive had taken us almost an hour; the choosing about fifteen minutes; we still had plenty of time to do something else if we wanted. Did we want this non-date to continue? I did, but I was hesitant to bring up the idea of dinner because I felt like it was her place to make any suggestions. I'd already imposed myself on her errand. She was the one who'd cannily built the exit ramps.

"You want to get something to eat?" she said.

"Sure," I said, secretly rejoicing.

We stopped at a Thai place on the way back to town. The restaurant was perched on a cliff overlooking a powerful waterfall flowing past the ruins of an old paper mill. Under a heat shell on the patio, drinking iced tea and lemonade, we watched the water rage over the rocks, and I asked her more questions about her life: her friends, her family, her daily habits. She told me about her brother, who lived in Tacoma. She told me about her ladies' poker group that had been going for fifteen years straight. She told me about her morning routine of drinking hot water and lemon juice, a tiny act of self-care that carried her until at least lunchtime, self-care-wise.

"Then the self-care regimen is more like potato chips and champagne," she said. "That's my combo these days. Small pleasures."

"The best kind," I said.

I thought about telling her about my floundering Empty Chair story but decided against it, not wanting to seem too work-obsessed. Instead, we burrowed into the past again and talked about some of our old friends, reliving some of the old controversies. Our attitudes hadn't really changed, it seemed. What had seemed wrong then seemed wrong now. What had seemed fine seemed fine. What had seemed ambiguous still seemed ambiguous and still seemed worth talking over.

We finished dinner by 7:30 p.m., and again, we faced a decision. We were done with dinner, but did we have the desire to go even longer? Personally, I hoped we did, and I got the feeling Sobie felt the same way, judging from the winding path she took getting us back to the city. She puttered down the main road, taking side streets into neighborhoods she claimed she wanted to scout, generally dawdling at every opportunity. But as slowly as we progressed, the night was still drawing to an end.

At last, we reentered the lights and relative bustle of the city, and I made some suggestions that would extend our time together. We could go to a movie. Or a concert. Or rock climbing at the gym. But none of the ideas appealed. They were all too onerous or boring or ruined by whatever new technological improvement had been forced onto the world. We both seemed to want to close out the night with a little flair, but neither of us could think of what that might be.

"What about laser tag?" Sobie said. "I've never tried that before."

"Me neither," I said.

"Aren't there real shootings in those places, though?" she said. "People really kill each other?"

"I don't think that's happening anymore," I said. "That was more like 2040, '41."

"I can't be out too late," she said. "I have things I have to do in the morning."

"I don't think the games last that long," I said.

"Well," she said, and seemed to give the idea a final, hard think. "Nothing's happening tonight, physically, just so you know."

"Of course," I said.

"I take things a lot slower now," she said. "I've learned some things."

"We're just talking about laser tag," I said. "Then home."

She turned the car at the next intersection and drove us directly to the nearest parlor. We paid our fee and did our training module, and within minutes we were donning our goggles and entering the gaming chamber. Minutes after that, we were dealing out laser shocks to little children and stoned teenagers alike. I became a cyber-monk patrolling a Han-era temple, and she a priestess-warrior in Machu Picchu 3000. Together, we laid waste to the incoming Huns and invading alien conquistadors. Chasms grew in the earth underneath us. Ogres spurted orange blood. My sky filled with golden, hyper-articulated dragons, and hers with robot pterodactyls. For four game cycles, we wantonly slayed our enemies by the dozens, and still we managed to make it home by 10:00.

4

Why did Liu change his mind? Some wind blew into his ear, some cloud talked to him. He ate a banana and his blood sugar jumped and a pathway opened from his nervous system into his prefrontal cortex. I thought of him as a giant hunk of meat with senses that blinked on and off depending on the light and heat, generating orders that had almost nothing to do with any kind of reason. But under the skin it often turned out there was some kind of logic at work. He did manage to keep a lot of people employed.

At Aliyah's urging, he'd agreed at least to send Jeff's video in for vocal analysis. It'd come back with a 73 percent probability of a match, which was to say there were some glottal similarities and shared vowel intensities with the extant recordings of Robert Cave, but nothing that could be considered a perfect acoustic fingerprint, and nothing to hang a story on, let alone anything that would hold up in court. The spectrogram with its bar graphs and the interesting phonatory deviation diagrams might have edged Liu closer to reconsideration, but none of it really explained the change of mind.

Aliyah suspected it was his wife, Hannah. Hannah was often lurking somewhere in the background of Liu's decision-making process, such as it was, feeding him opinions, bending his thoughts. She was by all accounts a wicked, vengeful person, very funny, and probably relished the idea of smiting the prime Denier Cave from afar. If the *Globe* revealed his identity to the world, she could brag about her role at the City Club for the next ten years. That was Aliyah's theory, anyway.

Once Liu made a decision, everything became a major rush. One day I was riding the bus, the next I was booking airplane tickets, packing, and getting my house in order for an open-ended absence. Thankfully, I didn't have a dog or cat or even much in the way of houseplants to abandon, so the house part wasn't hard. This was why I lived as simply as I did: so I could always just go. Not that I very often did.

I also had to update my digital alias, which meant adding entries to one of my stripped-down portfolios. In the past, I'd cast myself as an adman with a broken marriage, a contractor with a music-recording hobby, or an unemployed PR agent, depending on the tale I was spinning, with pictures of myself at birthday parties and on vacations swapping out in all the threads. This time, inspired by Sobie, I fashioned myself a real estate investor, hunting for a new personal vacation spot south of the border. I figured real estate was a subject everyone wanted to talk about and would explain my appearance on any number of tangents. I spent a few hours uploading fresh posts and time-stamped videos to the storyline. The shell was only a few layers deep, but the identity scanned as long as no one got too curious.

I didn't have time to see Sobie before I left, but we talked a few times on the phone. I wasn't at liberty to tell her much about my assignment, as the *Globe* wanted everything very hush-hush, but that didn't keep her from guessing. I gave her leading yes and no answers for the most part, and if she grazed too close to important information, I responded with silence, as if silence were somehow neutral.

"Is it a work trip?"

"Yeah."

"Is it in this country?"

"No."

"This hemisphere?"

"Yeah."

"Spanish-speaking?"

No answer.

She figured out the general outline of my mission pretty quickly but thankfully backed off before I had to lie.

"I'm jealous," she said. "Mexico sounds great. Sun would be really nice right now."

"It's not coastal," I said. "I'm going to a city."

"The biggest city?"

"No."

"Second-biggest?"

Silence.

"Well, that sounds great, too. Everything sounds good. How long do you think you'll be gone?"

"I actually have no idea."

We weren't at a place where we could tell each other we cared one way or another whether I was gone for a long time or not. We'd managed to get by without each other's company for two and a half decades and counting. The last thing I wanted was to rattle her by telling her I'd be thinking about her while I was away, and she didn't want to tell me she'd be thinking of me, either. Which meant there wasn't much more to say than good luck.

*   *   *

My flight went through Dallas, a red-eye. I arrived in Guadalajara at sunrise. Stepping out of the terminal, I could smell smoke in the air from the wildfires burning to the northwest, spreading over the grasses and scrub brush of five hundred square miles. I smelled notes of mesquite and other, more acrid scents, too— burned rubber, charred metal. Driving out of the airport, the sun rising through the brightening haze, I saw wild dogs scavenging in a vacant lot. I felt like I was a wild dog, roaming the plains to feed on the entrails of rumor, hearsay, and shit information.

I checked into the Best Western on Calle Ortega well before noon. My room was on the third floor overlooking a side street with a few low apartment buildings and a pothole in the middle of the road the size of a grave. At the center of the block was a torta stand surrounded by many worn plastic buckets. I could see a tamarind tree shading the greasy dirt of an auto body shop, and in the lot, a few men staring at phones. The sound of a two-stroke engine skipping a cog circled somewhere in the neighborhood.

The room came with a mild dampness and a heavy-duty pineapple air-freshener scent. I didn't want to be in there any longer than I had to, and I was too wired to rest, so as soon as I'd dumped my bags, I went out in search of Cave's block.

I'd selected the Best Western for its proximity to Cave's supposed address, and within fifteen minutes I was on the corner of the presumed street. The houses there were humble, but the electrified fences suggested a wealthy district, as did the three large jacaranda trees casting luxuriant shade. The buildings were mostly cinder block, two stories, the front yards sad aprons of dirt or dusty concrete.

I sat on a bench for an hour holding a book. It was the first book I'd grabbed from my shelf, *The Adventures of Huckleberry Finn*, something I'd been meaning to reread for many years. Mostly I used it as a mask, but as often as I looked up from the pages, no one even slightly resembling Robert Cave passed by. The smoke continued to hover overhead, making jaundiced halos shot with shadows around the buildings and antennae. The sky was a shifting scale of taupe, beige, and near-mustard. My skin looked like burned tapioca in the light.

In the early afternoon, I decided to head to the museum, which wasn't that far. By the time I got there, a wreath of smog had descended to ground level, and in the thickening ash and grit, the old colonial edifice appeared like a gray specter over the congested street.

I paid at the door and headed down the cool, tiled breezeway, passing a verdant courtyard garden overflowing with orchids, agave, and crenulated succulents. The café was in the corner of the building and turned out to be a large, high room with long rafters crossing the stucco ceiling. At the counter the teenage barista from the video presided over three customers nursing cups of coffee. It was a quiet room. It smelled good. The light was nice.

I ordered a cup of coffee and sat at a table against a wall, nodding off immediately. The travel was finally hitting me. I roused myself and tried to read again, finding Huck fooling around under a bridge, eavesdropping on some ornery townspeople, but I dozed off again before the chapter ended, succumbing to the delicious torpor.

Late in the afternoon, the room picked up a few more sitters and lost them again. None were Cave. At five o'clock, the museum closed, and I had to wander off, sluggish and numb from the napping. I staggered back to the hotel and promptly left again. I'd dozed for too long, and the charge of travel was running through my nerves, keeping me on the move.

I wandered the blocks surrounding the hotel, taking wider and wider circuits through the neighborhood. The streets of Guadalajara were messy but functional, and the people seemed lively and urbane, dressed like city people anywhere. I passed small bookstores, fragrant bakeries, and colorful ice cream shops with posters for bullfights in the windows. Lean matadors coaxed giant bulls using sweeping magenta capes. I passed the same squalid shanties we had up north, filled with the same desperate, destitute refugees. Men and women sprawled asleep, nodding off, crusted in grime, ranting. I passed a broken fence overtaken by wild grasses. In a park, I came to a woman doing magic tricks inside a giant, scuffed plastic ball. It was supposed to be a crystal ball, I realized, and placed a dollar in her plate.

*   *   *

I got back to the hotel and slept. In the morning, I woke to the sound of roosters. I made instant coffee I'd brought from home and read the headlines of the day, keeping my normal routine. At 9:00 a.m., opening time, I went to the museum to stake out Cave. I was using the logic of a person lost in the woods: choose a tree and stay put. Help would come if you kept still and didn't panic.

I paid my admission, ordered another coffee, and took my seat near the window where I could see the traffic and a stretch of the sidewalk running alongside the armory building. I could watch the pedestrians shuffling across the intersection with the lights and distant bright clouds creeping across the sky, heading elsewhere. The smoke was gone, at least for the morning.

The coffee was fine. I read the news again in more detail. There'd been a mass sardine die-off in Greece, and in Ireland, a small startup had engineered a synthetic protein with real smoked-ham taste. Within an hour, I'd consumed all the news and the commentary about the news, and I was back to reading my book. Huck was escaping the terror of his alcoholic father by slaughtering a pig and spreading the blood all over the cabin in order to fake his own death. It was quite a scheme.

Every few minutes, I looked up in the hopes that Cave would appear, but there was no sign of him. The light gradually edged across the walls, dragging the leaf shadows over the café's framed exhibition posters. The barista bused the tables and returned to her post, bused and returned. I wasn't in any hurry now. This was the part of the job I savored, the waiting. If I'd been in the café on vacation I might have felt anxious. I might have felt like I was supposed to be doing something, going somewhere. But as it was, I knew exactly where I was supposed to be, which conferred the waiting with a kind of calm. The sound of the barista replacing the silverware in her drawers was only relaxing. So this was what a spider felt like in its web.

Cave didn't show in the morning. And he didn't show after lunch.

Midafternoon, I started making forays into the galleries of the Regional Art Museum of Guadalajara. It was a kind of

flea market, I found, with random bits of everything in the vit-
rines: samples of Colima's red pottery, necklaces, lip ornaments,
bracelets, ear spools, and pectorals made of bone, shell, seeds,
and stones. They had a fiberglass replica of a meteorite that had
struck near Zacatecas twenty thousand years ago, and a few
paintings by Murillo, one attributed to Brueghel. Through all the
buffeting storms of history, somehow, these objects had remained
inside these walls, protected.

I kept on the ground floor, wanting to stick close to the café
just in case. In the main gallery were skeletons of a rhinoceros
and a saber-toothed tiger, unburied from somewhere nearby, and
the big-ticket item: the skeleton of a mastodon dating from the
Pleistocene. The bones described the whole animal—giant tusks,
giant femurs, giant ribs, all of it—pulled intact from a muddy
swamp somewhere. I enjoyed staring at the bones. It was hard
to imagine this creature had ever walked the earth.

As I stared at the mastodon I tried to imagine its world.
What a pulsating, magical orb it must have been, crazed with
budding life. I imagined myself as a humanoid figure walking
in that ecosystem, an ancient man with unshaven cheeks and
muscular arms and legs. I imagined walking in the jungle, fearful
of every feathered, scaly, fanged predator. I gave myself a jade
knife and pushed through the rubbery leaves, brushing away the
pink, pouting flowers and the hanging vines.

I imagined coming to a stream crowded with fish. Their scales
slid under the surface, forming a silvery frieze. From the trees

expanded a cloud of birds that grew and grew until the sky was dark with wings. Birdsong crashed down for miles. And then, in a meadow, this thing appeared, this wizened woolly mammoth feeding on pampas grass. I could smell it all the way across the landscape, its stench of sweat and fur, dried shit, hot breath. Beyond the mastodon, the forest rolled to a jagged mountain range, and beyond the mountains, empty sky—the infinite diorama of the prehistoric world. And then, as quickly as it came, my fantasy retracted. I was back in the gallery, alone.

*   *   *

I left the museum just before closing and went to a cantina on Cave's street, hoping for some kind of blind luck. The cantina was phenomenal in its mediocrity. They served nuts powdered with some green dust and lukewarm Bohemia beer. There were no other gringos in the place, and I felt like the locals couldn't even see me. The language barrier was like a two-way mirror. I couldn't understand them; they couldn't understand me; we mutually didn't exist.

I was back at the hotel by nine o'clock. Again, I couldn't sleep, so I got up and paced around like an animal. I watched TV, ate candy. I wasn't used to being alone for so long. I had the first quiver of intestinal problems. I was already getting more accustomed to the scent that permeated my clothes and stuck in my hair. It was part of my life now.

I wrote to Sobie, "I'm here. I'm bored."

"More boring here," she wrote back.

At ten o'clock, I went downstairs and tried talking to the guy at the desk. He had a big potbelly and bizarre flocking in his hair. It looked like he'd spray-painted his head with black aerosol. I tried asking about "interesting things to do at night," but it was almost impossible to get my meaning across. What did I like to do? Musica? Películas? Sure, no. We engaged in a halting back-and-forth, trying to understand each other and failing repeatedly, and when he tried to interest me in a date with his sister, I left to find other distractions.

I wandered into the neighborhood around the hotel, which was partly a tourist neighborhood, partly financial, partly residential, and also none of those things. I passed college kids smoking on a wall, a dog with a huge cyst on its neck, a boy eating from a plastic bag filled with cereal and milk and hot sauce. I walked down a street of cars with portable hibachis in their trunks selling corn, chicken, and tamales, my mouth watering, but I didn't dare.

I ended up in a public square crowded with people of all ages. The older people were dressed in suit jackets and tulle dresses, promenading in couples. The children were running around barefoot, in gangs, playing trumpets and kazoos. In the center of the square were about a dozen kids shooting glow-in-the-dark hand rockets in the air. The rockets were plastic glosticks wrapped around plastic projectiles, launched by plastic slingshots, flying up and floating to earth on plastic propellers. They were built to last only a matter of hours, objects we'd banned up north years ago.

I sat on a bench and watched the scene of the kids launching their toys into the air and waiting for them to float back down to earth. They shrieked and ran around trying to catch them before they touched. How many eons would it take for the world to digest these things? I wondered. How many years before someone dug them up and put them in a museum?

5

Within three days, the barista had learned my order. I arrived at opening time, took my seat, and a few minutes later she brought it over on a little wooden tray—a cup of Mexican mocha with a sprinkle of nutmeg and cayenne, a glass of filtered water, and a banderilla, a long, skinny pan dulce drizzled with caramelized glaze.

Cave walked in on day four. I didn't notice him at first. I was drinking my second cup of coffee, reading *Huckleberry Finn*, and when I looked up, there he was, ordering his drink at the counter. I recognized him not only from Jeff's video but from the hundreds of images I'd peeled from the digital record by that point. I'd seen his face in magazine profiles, publicity pictures, and the archives of his scattered family and friends. I'd seen footage of him delivering valedictory lectures in distinguished gowns, striding in a power suit under whipping helicopter blades, and working the grill at a company retreat in Connecticut. I'd seen him from

every angle, at every time of the day, in every season, with almost
every publicly acceptable emotion lining his features, from noble
concentration to forced hilarity to genuine, overflowing affection.
And then, post-2032, the feed disappeared, the record stopped.

Now here he was, the soft, living flesh, the object of all those
flat pictures, the source. The thrilling disappointment of seeing
a famous person in their natural setting ran through me—the
meager physical body replacing the photographic record—and
then, rapidly, something colder, more appraising.

Cave was a tall, thin man. His skin was pale. His hair was
white. He wore it closely cropped around the temples so his
large, wrinkled ears dangled free and a little lengthy in the bangs,
which he swept over to the side. He had a serious forehead, small,
inset eyes, and a puggish nose. He had a stretched upper lip, a
thin, wry mouth, and a once-strong chin that had become dented
and creased with age. He didn't wear the chinos and sweatshirt of
the average American retiree, but something more sophisticated
and bespoke—a blue, open-collared oxford under a fitted sport
coat and dark slacks, with polished, Italianate loafers. On his left
hand was a large golden ring with a flat pink stone. His fingers
themselves were thin but swollen-knuckled. He was seventy-
seven years old but still held on to a certain spectral virility.

The barista seemed happy to see him, and they joked around
while she made his café de olla, a coffee drink with such insane
amounts of cinnamon and sugar it never fully ungranulated. Cave
partly bowed when the cup entered his hands and transported

the hot vessel to a table across the room with a shuffling step. I watched out of the corner of my eye as he swiped off a few crumbs. He placed his cup, sat down, and started reading the *New York Times* on his digipaper.

He moved with loose, unhurried deliberation. He sipped; he slid his finger across the page; he rested his finger on his lip. For now, my only goal was positive identification. When the time came, I knew, he might deny his own image, his own DNA, which meant the more airtight our documentation, the better. To that end, I'd already begun recording him, snapping time-stamped pictures with the camera embedded in my glasses. It was a good camera, 58mm lens, strong zoom, synching constantly with my phone, which synched with my cached memory files. Everything I saw and heard would go to Aliyah for authentica-tion when I got back to the hotel.

Cave smoothed his digipaper and folded it in half, poring over the sports section. It was almost unseemly how much I enjoyed watching him. He had no idea what story was beginning to encircle him. I could almost see the manacles of justice crawl-ing his way, fitting themselves to his fine, liver-spotted wrists and ankles. Pretty soon the real camera would arrive, and then he'd be carted off to a cell in The Hague, or possibly Toronto, I wasn't sure where. Among all the people in the world, in this moment, only I knew his fate.

I made a show of reading *Huckleberry Finn*, but I couldn't concentrate. I kept rereading the same paragraph, something about moonlight on the Mississippi. Between sentences I raised my eyes and collected more images. I wasn't in any rush.

When Cave finished his cup of coffee he went back to the counter for a refill, and I casually rose and took a place behind him. I was hoping to collect some clean audio, but unfortunately he didn't joke around with the barista this time. He just said, "Un otro, por favor," and stepped aside to make room for the next customer, me. The espresso machine sounded, just like in Jeff's video, and Cave stood there idly, waiting.

I ordered "uno más" and waited while the barista toiled on both our drinks at once, banging her espresso scoop and operating the steam valves. I could feel Cave's presence a few feet away, but I didn't want to look at him and give him any reason to wonder about me. I could collect his voice on another round, I thought. It didn't even have to be today. He was obviously a regular at the café, just like Jeff had promised. We'd be speaking soon enough.

But then it turned out I didn't have to wait.

"Good book," Cave said. He was reaching for his espresso and addressing me out of the corner of his eye, raising a friendly eyebrow.

"Hmm?" I said. I doubted he was talking to me at first, but as no one else was around, I couldn't ignore him.

"Good book," he said again. He nodded over at my table, where *Huckleberry Finn* was resting cover up, the title legible for anyone to see. "Good to see someone reading a book."

"Yes," I said, and sensing that wasn't enough, added, "I thought I'd give it a try. It's been a while. It's a good one." I did my best to sound natural, like I was just another ordinary customer in the museum coffee shop, not a predator stalking him like a gazelle.

"Sure is," he said. He ripped off the end of a sachet of sugar and poured the brown granules into his cup. He had a sweet tooth. They never mentioned that in his profiles. He started stirring and I assumed our conversation had run its course, but he surprised me again, saying, "This is strange. Hold on."

I waited as he walked to his table and reached into a hand-tooled leather bag hanging on the back of his chair. He felt around inside the bag and withdrew a hardcover book and turned around and walked back toward me. The book looked to be an old library copy, without a dust jacket, pale green. He handed it over. The cover was blank and frayed, so I turned it to read the faded gilded lettering on the spine. It was *The Adventures of Tom Sawyer*.

"Oh," I said. "That is strange."

"Isn't it?"

We stood in silence, aware that some synchronicity had occurred. The warm, fragrant café seemed to pulse with unseen energies. Here we were, two gringos in a museum coffee shop in Guadalajara, both reading Mark Twain novels. What were the chances? It was one of those bizarre but not unheard of, not even that uncommon, serendipities that decorated the experience of a life, and in journalism tended to cluster around a good hunch.

"I never read this one," I said, handing the book back.

"I've been reading a lot of Twain lately," Cave said. His voice was surprisingly youthful. "Some of them are amazing. Some of them are pretty sloppy, to be honest. He was really cranking it out, you know? But the good ones, boy, they hold up. A lot of his sentences, they have that marble-mouthed backwoods Americana thing going on, but most of them could be written today."

"I bet," I said.

"I like reading them on paper, too," he said, lightly tapping the binding. "The whole smell of a book, the physical weight. I don't think you get the full experience on a screen. Even these soft screens. I can read the newspaper on those, they're good for that, but not for a book. A book is a perfect technology."

Cave was leaning toward me now, practically breathing in my face with his enthusiasm. When he smiled, he showed his yellow teeth. Whatever suspicion he should have felt toward me had been canceled by the twinned books. Again, I wasn't sure what would seem natural on my end, so I said nothing.

"I found this copy at the mercado," he said. "They had a complete Twain collection from an elementary school in Kansas. I thought they should stay together, so I bought the whole stack. I've been revisiting old things lately. I'm at that age." He gave a little trill of irony at the mention of his age. "You're liking that one all right?"

"Very much," I said.

"There's a scene in there, early on, that I found quite incredible," he said. "It wasn't much. Huck and Jim are just getting out on the river. They're in hiding, so they're floating at night and sleeping in the day, and when the night is almost over they tie up and have a swim. They sit down together on the sandy bottom where the water is about knee-deep and watch the sun rise. It isn't a very long section. Nothing happens. Everything is silent, perfectly still. Bullfrogs clattering. But it's just a fantastic passage.

"I mean, just think about that," he went on. "Huckleberry Finn is a white thirteen-year-old boy. Jim is a Black middle-aged man. They're sitting there in the river, naked, peacefully enjoying the sunrise. What an image! You think about it as an image and it really boggles your mind, doesn't it? You'd have trouble explaining that picture if you saw it, even today."

"That's true," I said. "You would."

"It's really something," he said, sipping his coffee with satisfaction. "I'm glad I'm not the only one with it in my head."

Cave didn't exactly ask me to join him, but something in his posture implied an invitation, and without any explicit agreement, we drifted over and took the seats at his table. It seemed like a big risk for a person hiding from the law, but already I was starting to understand he was more starved for conversation than anything else. He'd been in exile for almost twenty years, after all. In that time, he'd probably encountered hundreds if not thousands of people who'd failed to put his face to his name, and he'd gradually moved beyond paranoia into something like his natural, amiable state of personality. His profiles often talked about his niceness, his good humor. At this point, his affability was probably even part of his disguise. He was a purloined letter of a criminal Denier refugee, hiding in plain sight, seeing no threats and thus no threats seeing him. I didn't blame him for missing some of the small, normal interactions of life.

"There are a lot of books I missed when I was younger," he said, his elbows on his knees, leaning in to the talk. "They weren't really teaching Twain when I was a kid. Which made perfect sense. Twain can take care of himself. I'm not worried about Twain. But it turns out there's something about him that stays interesting. I suppose that's why he's a figure of history at this point. His whole life is kind of emblematic of something. Did you know that he served as a Confederate soldier in the Civil War as a young man?"

"No," I said.

"And that he ended as a vehement anti-imperialist during the Spanish-American War?"

"I did know that," I said.

"And that he abandoned a book called *Huck Finn and Tom Sawyer Among the Indians*?"

"I didn't know that, either."

"Quite a life," he said. "In and out with Halley's Comet. He even predicted his own death based on that astronomical event. 'The Almighty has said, no doubt: Now here are these two unaccountable freaks; they came in together, they must go out together.' I love that phrasing, 'two unaccountable freaks.' What a life," Cave said, shaking his head. "What a life!"

Like everybody, Cave was interested in the racial dimensions of *Huckleberry Finn*.

"There are things about Jim's character that are just unquestionably degrading," he said, sipping his coffee. "You can't deny that. He's servile, he's credulous, he's superstitious. Some of it, you're just: oof, no thank you. But I'd argue there's something else going on in there, too. Something that keeps bringing Jim back into the realm of humanity. You can almost feel Twain straining inside the limits of his times, don't you think?"

"I guess so," I said.

"To me, that's what's fascinating about *Huckleberry Finn*," he said. "Watching Twain writing himself into a deeper understanding of who he is, of what America is. Following the language until he can't deny Jim's humanity any longer. A person can only get so far outside their moment, granted, but Twain's really doing something in there.

"Not that his friend Frederick Douglass ever would have questioned Black people's humanity in the first place," he said. "So I guess we can only give Twain so much credit for that! But you know, Frederick Douglass and Mark Twain, that's its own incredible story. They were on the lecture circuit together. Douglass actually attended a public reading of *Huckleberry Finn* . . ."

The longer we talked, the stranger the whole conversation became. Cave had a professorial air and seemed to enjoy the sound of his own voice and the pleasure of capturing his own complex sensibility in words. He listened on occasion, but not that closely, and mostly only in order to seize on something I said and pivot back into his own storytelling. He seemed to have a lot of thoughts piled up that he wanted to share. I thought I caught the whiff of something tragic in his perceptions, something romantic, almost operatic. He definitely seemed aware of his own pretentious manner. He laughed at himself, forgave himself easily. But for all his enthusiastic digressions, all his learned musings, he remained somehow impervious, too, unreachable. Knowing the crimes he'd perpetrated, the fires still burning around the globe, I couldn't help but find him almost diabolical. I didn't see that his guilt weighed on him at all.

By the end of our forty-five-minute conversation I had plenty of audio in my pocket. I'd been recording the whole time, capturing every syllable. As we rose and said our goodbyes, gathering our phones and books into our respective packs, we finally went over some basic information that we'd skipped at the beginning.

"So you're down here on vacation?" he said politely.

"I might be looking to buy something, actually," I said. "I've been hearing good things about Guadalajara. I'm kind of on a scouting mission. Seeing what the city has to offer."

"You're looking at a good time," he said. "Not a lot of North Americans moving down here these days. They think it's a wasteland. They think everyone's living in caves. They have no idea."

"It seems like a beautiful city," I said.

"It's a gorgeous city," he said. "Not second fiddle to Mexico City at all. If you've got time, you should visit the Providencia neighborhood. Some very charming streets over there. That's where a lot of the Europeans and Brazilians are landing these days, I hear."

"I will," I said. "So I guess you've been living here a long time?"

"Quite a while," he said.

"And you're from the States originally?" I said.

"Among other places," he said.

"I'll check out *Tom Sawyer*," I said.

"You'll like it," he said. "My name's Bob, by the way." He extended his hand. "Bob Beck."

"Jake," I said. "Jake Henry."

"Good to meet you, Jake," he said. "Always nice to meet another book lover." And we shook hands, two readers far from home, two liars who'd found a magnet of truth.

6

I sent the visual and audio files directly to Liu and Aliyah. Aliyah
sent them in for analysis, which would take a few days to come
back. In the meantime, we decided I should keep my distance
from the museum. The rabbit was in our sights, we agreed. Now
was the time to hold the stock and cock the hammer in silence.

Until then, we had plenty of logistics to work out. What was
the best way to drag a person out of the underground and into
the klieg lights of history? What was the best way to expose a
double life? Even in a newsroom, this kind of problem didn't
present very often. At most, there were probably a few thousand
fugitives like Cave in the entire world—counting all the war
criminals, narco-traffickers, and mafia hit men stashed away in
the suburban homes and apartment buildings of normal society.
We had one. So now what?

In my hotel room, I'd already begun researching capture stories, looking for models for the outing. Who were our comps?

There was Aleksandras Lileikis, Lithuanian Nazi, arrested in 1994 in Boston by street cops; Ilija Josipovic, Bosnian Serb, arrested in 2017 in Akron by ICE for possessing fraudulent immigration documents; Jean Leonard Teganya, Rwandan serial rapist and murderer, arrested in 2019 by customs agents while walking across the border from Canada into Maine. There was even Eichmann himself, the granddaddy of them all, plucked from the streets of Argentina by Mossad agents and ferreted to Israel for show trial. But among all the historical examples of refugee captures on record, almost none of them, I found, involved journalists.

One case that did was that of Erich Priebke, an SS officer responsible for a mass killing in Italy in 1944. His victims included 335 Italian prisoners of war, some of whom were boys as young as fourteen, murdered in rows of five in the Ardeatine Caves outside Rome—a bullet to the back of each head, each row falling on the next. Priebke had organized the massacre and had been accused of killing at least two prisoners himself, but after the war he'd escaped to Argentina and taken up residence in the small mountain village of San Carlos de Bariloche in the foothills of the Andes. His wife and two sons had joined him in 1948, and for the next fifty years they'd lived together openly, under their own family name, as the proprietors of a small butcher shop.

Many of Priebke's neighbors had also been Nazis. They'd married each other, built Bavarian-looking restaurants together, buried each other in neighboring graves. As a community, they'd whiled away their lives in their mountain village, having children and grandchildren, laughing and eating together, letting the consequences of the twentieth century bead off their backs like water.

The idyll lasted until 1994, when the television reporter Sam Donaldson approached Priebke on the street with a camera crew. Priebke was wearing a silly German fedora and cardigan sweater that day, standing next to his yellowish Volkswagen. He had the affect of the jolly grandfather he was, his eyes twinkling, happy for the attention. The world had become populated by his offspring. The trees and the birds loved him. He couldn't believe that anyone might have a complaint about his life. Why would his grandchildren come for him in this way? The past was a dream.

"You live in this time," he said to Donaldson, "but we that lived in 1933"—he filled the ellipsis with a wave of the hand—"you understand that? Whole Germany was in it." He denied nothing.

By the end of the interview, however, Priebke wasn't so friendly anymore. "You are not a gentleman," he said, climbing into his Volkswagen and driving down the sunny street. A few months later, he was extradited to Italy. The trial went on for many years. He died in his cell in 2013, at the age of one hundred, of natural causes. He never accepted any responsibility for his actions during the war whatsoever.

I watched Donaldson's interview many times. I appreciated

his simple approach. The confrontation was undramatic, but it was all a person really needed. A camera and a certain unforgiving resolve. That was the beauty of a story like this. Only the facts were necessary. It took no style at all. One only had to get it down. Of course, Donaldson's piece had been the work of many months of preparation, with innumerable interns, producers, archivists, historians, and judicial experts contributing their labor, and the real journalists in the tale had been a producer named Harry Phillips and his entire investigative team, not the TV personality at all, but in the end it was very straightforward. Donaldson and a cameraman appeared on a street and proceeded to tear the old Nazi's life apart.

The conversation was remarkably unremarkable. If you didn't know better, it was just two old men talking on an alpine street. You could almost believe Priebke's claims of innocence in that moment, or at least the inapplicability of the judgment of history. His life had sent him through multiple, incompatible realities. During the reality of his youth, a sickness had been rampant in the land, but thankfully the sickness had broken and the world had moved on. Ever after, he'd discharged his duties to family and community like any other decent citizen. How could he be judged for the actions of another lifetime now? They were the crimes of a different man. But Donaldson, to his credit, refused to forget.

Through the whole interview, I wondered what was happening inside Priebke's head. What moral flaw had brought him to this place? And that moral flaw: Was it a flaw of fate or a flaw of his mind? Was it his own flaw or simply the circumstances of his time and place? What was the difference, ultimately, between him and me?

The answers were inaccessible, but in the small details you could catch a glimpse. In the little details, the soundlessness of truth came through, so limited but so real. Priebke's hat. The car keys in his hand. The way he rolled his head to turn away and then turned back again in the same motion to face the camera. Those were the kinds of details I wanted from Cave. We might never know what went on in his soul, but we could know the coffee he drank, the style of ring he wore. From those facts we could build some kind of understanding.

Listening to Cave's voice flowing from the speaker in my hotel, I began to understand we'd been granted an opportunity. Unexpectedly, two books had appeared in a room. In the grand spectrum of events, it was a fairly average coincidence, significant or accidental, depending on interpretation. But in this case, the coincidence had practical value. Simply by appearing, the books had sparked Cave's interest in me. They'd transformed me from a potentially threatening adversary into a potentially pleasant conversational companion. And as such, if I wanted to collect more details about Cave's life and mind—not to understand him, I told myself, but only to describe him—the door was open.

I talked to Aliyah about it, and she agreed.

"Absolutely," she said. "When you put it that way, it's a sign. You should go talk to him again."

"I'm not saying a sign," I said. "I'm saying more like a tool."

"Okay," she said. "Either way."

"You think Liu would be open to another meeting?" I said.

"Are you kidding me?" she said. "The spirit of Liu's dad visits him in the form of a hawk like every week. You know how the decisions get made around here. When the universe starts talking to you, Jack, I think you should listen. That's just how life works, if you're paying any kind of attention."

So it was decided. I'd go see Cave again. I'd engage him in another conversation. And the mercenary element of the decision we left unspoken. If the *Globe* wanted to profit off this story to the maximum degree, we all understood, the more content we harvested from Cave, the better.

*   *   *

I went to the museum the next day at lunchtime and took my regular spot. This time I didn't have to wait very long. Cave showed up midafternoon, entering the café with the same cheerful, proprietary air, in the same expensive leather loafers, wearing a long, camel-colored coat and a navy blue wool scarf. When he spotted me his face lit up. As soon as he'd sugared his drink, he came over to shake my hand.

"Afternoon," he said. "You're back. The reader."

"It's such a good place to sit," I said, closing my book. "So quiet. Such a good place to think."

"Isn't it?" he said. "Just don't tell anyone. We don't want it overrun with tourists."

I asked him to have a seat and he gladly obliged, unwinding his scarf and stuffing it in his pocket. We traded small talk for a while about house hunting, the market in Mexico, the arduous struggle to find exactly the right place to live. The shock of our Twain connection had already dimmed, but thankfully it had left a residue, a warmth, and we were able to wander the pathways of average conversation with a little extra kick. I could ask him simple questions—What do you do in the city? How do you spend your time?—and he responded with openness and ease.

"There are trails in the mountains outside of the city," he said. "I like to hike on those whenever I can. The country is beautiful out there. The cacti are a whole botanical universe. They have such big personalities, all the agave, and the candelabra cactus. They're like people I go out and visit.

"The restaurants in Obrera are terrific," he said. "You have to like goat, though. I didn't know I would like goat so much. It was the Spanish who brought the goat to Mexico, you know. It's true. They were an invasive species. The goat took over the whole country. The soup here, birria, is Jalisco's solution to the goat problem."

He had a small life, he said. He enjoyed his routine. He had a weekly schedule that moved him between his home, the museum, the gym, the market, his studio.

His studio? I asked.

"Oh, it's nothing," he said.

"No, no, I'm curious," I said. "What kind of studio?"

"I'm at that age," he said, crossing his arms and leaning back, regaling me. "I've started painting, if you can believe it. I was an engineer my whole career, and now I paint. I can't believe I wasted my whole life not painting."

He was more than happy to tell me about his art.

"I like to paint simple things," he said. "People, animals, landscapes. I'm old-fashioned that way. I'm not very good at it, but it turns out I love the whole atmosphere of painting. I like the quiet of the studio, the smell of the paint. I like listening to the radio for a few hours at a time. I like oils, but I think I'm starting to prefer gouache.

"Gouache is a lot like watercolors," he said. "The particles are bigger, and the ratio of pigment to binder is higher, so it ends up looking more opaque, with more reflective qualities. But the thing I like about gouache is the same as watercolors. You have to work fast and not make any mistakes. Or you have to learn how to turn the mistakes into positives. The paint has its own ideas. It's a very forgiving medium, in other words, and for a painter of my quote unquote talents, I need that kind of forgiveness."

He asked me a few questions, too, but they were easy to deflect. Mostly, he enjoyed doing the talking. He seemed to think it was his job to entertain me. I pushed us easily into the subject of his past.

He said his dad had been in the army, and he'd grown up all over the world. He'd lived in ten states by the time he was eight, and he'd gone to five high schools on four continents. College in Madison, Wisconsin, was the longest he'd ever lived in one city up to that point, and he'd exited with a degree in hydro-engineering. He'd started traveling again for his career as soon as he graduated.

He'd specialized in airports, he claimed, and here the conversation began taking on a stereoscopic effect, as his cover story diverged from the biography I knew from the public record. He said he'd specialized in the plumbing systems at airports. Which airports? I asked. If I'd used a bathroom at the terminal at Denver International, that was him, he said. Pipes were his game, connecting the new physical plants to the municipal waterworks.

I pushed a little further, and he had answers well-formed and handy. Every year was accounted for. He'd left the US in his late fifties, he said, having done a pretty good job of investing and knowing his money would last longer in Mexico. The Upheavals had rendered his professional life obsolete anyway. There would be no more large-scale building projects happening that decade. He'd been sorry to give up his work, but it had all turned out for the best. He loved Mexico. He still had a small group of friends he stayed in touch with, scattered around the world, and they sent each other letters, but he'd come to embrace the solitude of his Mexican existence.

"You don't miss the States at all?" I said.

"No," he said. "Not at all."

"So no family up there anymore?" I said, probing. "You don't ever visit?" I was looking for the edges of his disguise, wondering if it rebonded with his actual life at any point or if his fabricated biography went all the way to the margins of his existence.

"I had a wife," he said, "but we divorced. We don't talk." This was true. His wife had become a lawyer for Greenpeace after Toronto. She'd remarried a lawyer for an investment banking firm. They lived in Delaware.

"No kids?" I said.

"No."

This was false. Cave had a son who'd been institutionalized in his twenties. He emerged sometimes from the fog of antipsychotics to write long public diatribes against his father and his father's crimes against the planet. He'd even sold the rights of his life story to a television production company, though nothing had come of the project. I wasn't sure what to make of Cave's denial of his own son. Maybe it was an act of mercy on his part, or self-protection, or wish fulfillment, I'd never know. Maybe it just raised too many questions. In any case, I had it on tape.

I could tell we'd grazed close to an edge of something because Cave deftly brought us back into the more comfortable terrain of Guadalajara's many touristic charms. He wanted to know if I'd been to the Museum of the Arts yet, or the Palacio de Gobierno, or any of the galleries. The art world of Guadalajara was much more interesting than people thought, he said, not second fiddle to Mexico City at all. Already, I was starting to hear his pet phrasings for a second time.

"And I assume you've been to the Hospicio Cabañas," he said.

"No," I said. "What is that?"

He shook his head at my delightful ignorance. "José Orozco painted the frescos there," he said. "It's his masterpiece. He painted them all freehand, without a backing sketch. It is phenomenal. You have to see it while you're here."

"I definitely will," I said.

He looked at his watch. He drummed his fingers with their fat knuckles once on the table and seemed to think about his coming obligations.

"It's only a ten-minute walk," he said. "Are you interested? I'm always ready to go."

"Of course."

*   *   *

We gathered up our things and walked to the Hospicio Cabañas, which was a straight shot down Avenida República. Christmas had taken over the city, and giant shining ornaments and shaggy strands of tinsel hung on the facades of buildings and lampposts. The smoke in the air was pleasant smoke now, woodsmoke, like home, and people on the street bustled on holiday errands, carrying packages, buying paper bags of hot, roasted nuts. On the way, walking slowly, Cave told me all about the great painter

José Clemente Orozco, the greatest of all the great Mexican muralists, in his humble opinion.

"Born in 1883," he said. "In Ciudad Guzmán, not that far from here. His dad owned a soap factory and also edited for the local newspaper. His mom taught painting classes to the women of the neighborhood. Orozco liked to draw as a child, but when he was twenty-three he had an accident shooting off fireworks. He ended up with gangrene, and his entire left hand was amputated. So he became a painter with only one hand. I find that so interesting. The mark of destiny, you might say."

Orozco went on to become one of the three major muralists of Mexico, Cave said, alongside Diego Rivera and Orozco's art school classmate, David Alfaro Siqueiros. Orozco was the first of them to travel to America to establish his reputation, and he picked up a famous disciple, Jackson Pollock, along the way. He'd shown at MoMA. And then, as the world spiraled toward war and Mexico nationalized its oil industry, he'd returned to Guadalajara to paint his masterpiece.

"This is one of the reasons I stay in Guadalajara," he said. "This place has become a kind of church for me. I go every few months and just commune with it for a while. It always gives me something new. Here it is."

Already we'd arrived at the Hospicio Cabañas, another sooty gray eminence hemmed in by congested streets. After passing through the main gate we entered a classical complex of galleries and open courtyards, and as we arrived in the main plaza, I realized what Cave had been calling a hospital the whole time was in fact a chapel. Behind a row of simple arches rose the slightly menacing facade, topped by a dome on a cylinder of vaulted windows. Little stone turrets studded the dome's balustrade like frozen candle flames.

"Founded in 1791," Cave said. "Orozco painted it in 1937 or 1938. It's a designated UN historical site now. Shall we?"

We crossed the courtyard and entered the chapel's stony chill. The interior was impressive but not enormous, as far as cathedrals went. There was a short nave and a short transept that formed a cross centered on the main dome, all held together by beefy pillars that created a series of radiating bays. Every bay was covered in Orozco's paintings, his blazing, muddy orange, his charcoal black.

Cave had stopped talking, apparently wanting me to appreciate the paintings on my own terms. I drifted away, following my own eyes, understanding I was supposed to look intently and express my amazement. Cave might even be trying to tell me something, I thought. He was telling me something in the way that people tried to tell each other things they couldn't otherwise express.

The first thing I noticed about the frescoes was their harshness. After all these years, it looked like Orozco had vandalized the building, his style was so clearly pitched against the style of the supporting architecture. The chapel was straight colonialism, an expression of European godliness and scientific authority, and the paintings were aggressively Mexican—raw and folkloric.

There were no peaceful angels and cherubim on the walls. No single-point perspective leading to golden, resplendent thrones. It was like an explosion had happened, spraying the walls with colored shrapnel.

I drifted along the edges of the room and gradually the murals began to take on more meaningful shape. The subject was war. The entire chapel was a phantasmagoria of war, filled with scenes of brutal domination and carnage. A horse robot made of pistons and cogs, with a metal chain-link tail, galloping through an orange-skied battlefield. A two-headed horse with twin skeleton faces carrying a Spanish knight into a landscape of jumbled horse and man muscles. A tangled knot of swords and body parts pulsating violently.

I came to a pause at a gruesome Franciscan priest holding a crucifix over the head of a kneeling Indian. The crucifix's edges were sharpened like a sword, and at the priest's side was a banner carrying the first letters of the European alphabet.

"It's called *The Spanish Conquest of Mexico*," Cave said, appearing at my shoulder.

"Very dark," I said.

"Indeed," he said. "The formative event of modern Mexico. But Orozco wasn't only painting something about the past here. He was thinking about the wars of his own time, too. See how he's mixed together Mexico's Indians and Spain's monks and conquistadors and Germany's fascists and Russia's communists and America's capitalists into one big collage?"

We looked at the images together. It was true, the wars of many eras were overlapping.

"It's all one big war to him," Cave said. "But what I think is so interesting is how far back Orozco goes. He actually doesn't stop at the Spanish conquest of Mexico. His timeline goes all the way to the Aztecs. You see those sacrifices up there in the lunettes?"

He directed my eyes upward, to a series of images of monstrous Aztecs performing ceremonial murder at the base of an ancient pyramid.

"Yeah," I said.

"And down there, the gallery of dictators."

He nodded toward a painting of dictators preening before a parade of dehumanized marchers. The main dictator, puffed up with arrogance, had the face of a Toltec mask and wore colorful necklaces and arm bracelets. The other dictators, representing many races and nations, receded behind him in shadow, all leering.

"The Aztecs conquered the whole area around Mexico City two hundred years before Cortés landed," Cave said. "They sacrificed four hundred people a day sometimes. They were totalitarian monsters. That's what I find interesting about Orozco. He doesn't deny that history. He acknowledges that the imperialism and greed we associate with the West grows from this earth, too. He's the opposite of Rivera that way. For Rivera, the pre-Columbian world is a garden of Eden. It's all muscular priests and docile squaws living in perfect harmony. That's what people want to believe, I know, but it isn't true."

We began moving, taking in other scenes of bedlam, avoiding the handful of other visitors milling in the cathedral. As Cave mused aloud, I listened, recording all.

"Rivera is amazing," he said. "He's an encyclopedia. But he's vulgar underneath. He had one big idea, Communism, and it gave him the answer to everything. It unlocked the whole world. He was a fundamentalist that way. And Siqueiros was even worse. Did you know when Stalin signed the Ribbentrop Pact, Siqueiros edited out all the critiques of Fascism and Nazism from his work? Nazism reformed overnight. Truth warped with the party edict. He lived in the cult. Not Orozco."

We'd arrived at an image of Cortés, the conquistador, framed on a ceiling between four arches. He stared down at us wearing bulky, intimidating armor, with Frankenstein-like bolts at the joints and a gaping, empty chest cavity. In his right hand he held a bloody sword that dangled almost casually toward the ground, chopping an Indian peasant between the legs. The writhing brown bodies on the ground were mere torsos, truncated and squirming. Cortés didn't seem to notice them at all. He strode onward without remorse, kissed by an upside-down, blond angel.

"The Man," Cave said. "The Aztecs thought he was an emissary of Quetzalcoatl, or Quetzalcoatl himself. He killed Montezuma. Enslaved thousands. Killed millions. It boggles the mind, doesn't it? To come to a New World and assume it's yours to take."

"It does," I said.

"I wonder sometimes, though," he said, "what the ancient Polynesians would have done if they'd invented steel? They'd slaughter a low-caste person just for stepping in the headman's shadow. Or the Japanese if they'd invented guns and the intercontinental frigate ship? What kind of world empire would they have made? It might have been worse. I have a feeling it wouldn't have been much better. That's what Orozco is saying, I think. No one is not guilty on earth. No one is not implicated in the crime of living. I'm always amazed, looking at this mural. I just don't see any blind spots.

"Granted," he said, gazing on the vile Cortés, "some are more guilty than others."

We continued on, exploring the remaining vestibules and choirs, and finally came to a rest under the central dome. Painted into the eggshell of the cupola was a crucible of orange and yellow flame, surrounded by floating, death-gray men around the edges. At the center of the fire was a human figure either plummeting or rising, it was hard to say which. We were looking at him from below, at his feet, up the length of his flaming body, craning our necks.

"*The Man of Fire*," Cave said. "Prometheus overtaken by flames. That's how I read it, anyway. It's the Imagination. It's where Orozco sees any light. An immolating light, but still. You can't change how people are, I think he's saying, but you can illuminate their condition. You can say something true about how the world is.

"You asked if I ever wanted to go back to the States earlier," he went on, his eyes fixed on the ceiling. "I can't say I ever felt very rooted there, honestly, Jake. The history is so thin up in America. There are the cliff dwellings, and the mounds in the Midwest, but not the ancient dynastic history or structures you have down here. The pyramids, they change the whole mind frame. You go to Teotihuacán, or Palenque, you understand what a long continuum you're in. The temples at Teotihuacán, they're covered in dragons. You're in a relationship with China.

"It puts things in a different perspective," he said, still gazing upward. "Say what you will about America, Mexico is the center. I'm much happier here. I really am."

*   *   *

By the time we walked out of the hospicio the sun was setting. The wind was blustery, the Christmas lights were thrashing in the branches in the courtyard. I'd been recording everything, and I was eager to send the files to Aliyah. Cave hadn't exactly broken down in a tearful confession, but he'd given us something. I knew in some way we could use it.

Cave was putting on his coat and winding his scarf back around his neck, looking a little weary from all the walking and talking. We started our way down the stairs, leaning into the cold wind. I assumed our adventure was over and we'd say our goodbyes on the street, but as we began across the courtyard, he spoke through his upturned collar.

"I'm having dinner with my girlfriend," he said. "Did I mention her? We do fish night every Wednesday. I called her earlier and she says you should come over. If you'd like to, that is. No pressure at all. But if you're hungry, you're more than welcome."

7

Cave's girlfriend was named Maggie. Her apartment building was in the neighborhood of Providencia, another fifteen-minute walk. I'd passed through the neighborhood a few times on my nighttime rambles, and I'd wondered what went on inside the fortified homes and fenced-off garden restaurants. The zone was anchored by a vertical pod of Brutalist monoliths, though whether the pod was actual mid-twentieth-century Brutalist glass and concrete or an ersatz version built in the current century, I couldn't tell. The architectural times had gotten scrambled so long ago.

By the time we got there I'd learned a few things about Maggie. Her full name was Magdalene Deveraux, Cave had told me, which sounded French, but in fact she was Mexican. She was younger than Cave, around fifty, and they'd met ten years ago at an art gallery in Mexico City. She had degrees from Vassar and Columbia, and she'd grown up mostly in Rhode Island, but she made her living outside any nation-state whatsoever as a headhunter for elite medical institutions. Her niche was matching highly specialized doctors to research hospitals across Europe and South America, squashing viral outbreaks before they accelerated, which involved some extremely rarified forms of knowledge and customized search engines. The job meant strange hours and strange deadlines, but also big paydays, and allowed her to live and work wherever she pleased.

She'd joined Cave in Guadalajara five years ago. She'd rented her own apartment, and she'd kept her apartment in Mexico City, too. She had her own life, Cave felt the need to clarify, and she wasn't actually technically his girlfriend per se. He called her that to simplify matters, but they were both independent, individual people. They were more like companions, he said, coming and going as they chose but committed to their weekly dinner. The more he talked, the more I could see how important she was to him. So this was the life I'd be destroying.

Maggie was waiting for us when we got off the elevator, leaning out the doorway of her apartment at the end of the hallway, waving a bottle of champagne. Already, she was nothing like the person I'd expected from Cave's description. I'd imagined an imperious executive type, possibly with tasteful cosmetic surgery and a designer pantsuit. Or maybe a glamorous trophy blonde, in a golden kimono and platform mules. In fact, she was thickset and brassy and visibly drunk.

"Oh my God!" she said. "Finally! I'm starving! Come in! Come! Come! Get in here! The fish is going to dry out and blow away! Jesus fucking Christ."

Cave kissed Maggie on the cheek as he went in the door. "Mag, this is Jake," he said. "Jake, Mag. Jake's from the States. But he likes the café at the regional museum so much he might stay."

"Isn't that place amazing?" Maggie said. She drew out the word *amazing* in a way that made me unsure whether she was sincere. Was it amazing? Maybe so. I didn't have time to say one way or the other. "Bob could waste his whole life in there," she said. "And that mastodon. What an incredible beast! Imagine that thing's dong."

Cave made a sound of exasperation.

"What?" she said. "How can you look at it without thinking about that?"

"Somehow all these years I managed," he said.

"I don't believe you!" she said. "Everyone thinks about the mastodon's dong. That's the first thing you think of! Isn't that right, Jake? You agree with me."

"I couldn't really say," I said.

"Oh, you're just being polite," she said. "That's nice. You're a good guest. But you know it's true!"

*   *   *

The interior of Maggie's apartment was another surprise, causing another minor revision of opinion. It was immaculate, with a milky white carpet flowing to white walls illuminated by warm sconce lighting. A few widely spaced paintings and photographs hung above built-in bookshelves filled with thick art tomes and little pocket cubbies for sculptures and antique Native American baskets. Otherwise the room was empty, a study in negative space. On the far wall, twilight Guadalajara glittered in the window like a personal bauble.

Maggie led us across the tundra of carpet and took us to the kitchen, which turned out to be another immaculate room. The floor and walls were white porcelain tile. The refrigerator was canary yellow. The countertops were Mediterranean blue. And the fish—two raw, pink slabs gleaming with olive oil—sat on a silver cookie sheet beside a half-empty flute of champagne. Before anything, Maggie topped off her glass from her gold-foiled magnum.

"They said they didn't have the salmon from the farm we like," she said. "Those fuckers. I asked them a hundred times, 'Anything in the freezer? Back in the freezer? Hello?' I had to practically beg him to get him to go back in the freezer for me. I mean, really! Really! Is it so hard to go back and get a hunk of fish out of the freezer? You like salmon, don't you, Jake? I hope so."

"I do," I said.

"Well, you won't be getting that much tonight," she said. "Bobby called too late. I guess we'll cut them up somehow."

She leaned over and squinted at the fish. "Should I cut them up now, Bobby? Or after?"

"Easier to cut them after they cook," he said.

"But they'll fall apart then," she said. "And I have this incredible knife." She lifted a beautifully balanced cutting blade from the wooden block on the counter, swishing it thoughtlessly near her shoulder.

"Well, I don't know," he said, and they proceeded to debate the proper cutting technique for the fish. Now? After? And how should they cut the two pieces into three servings? It seemed best to cut a third off both pieces, for a total of four pieces, two large and two smaller, but which third should go? The back or the front?

They went around and around. Maggie became mildly frantic, arguing every side equally and Cave agreed with every position. Her energy was performative, I could tell, but at some point it occurred to me that my presence might actually be making her uncomfortable. Or maybe she was uncomfortable on Cave's behalf, I thought, worried he'd made a mistake in bringing me home. Or maybe she was only acting uncomfortable to make me feel more comfortable. I couldn't tell. Maybe she wasn't uncomfortable at all, and this was simply the way she acted. Whatever it was, Cave didn't seem to mind. He bantered, argued, gave in. We were down in the pocket of life now, apart from any politics or history, three people in a room figuring out dinner.

"Do you want anything to drink, Jake?" Maggie said, refilling her champagne glass again. "I should've asked you before. Bob's having beer, like a longshoreman."

"I am having beer," he said, pulling a brown bottle of porter from the refrigerator. "Maggie thinks beer is proletarian. But I like a beer on fish night."

"Beer," she said. "Disgusting. I can make you a martini, Jake. Or a boulevardier. Or a White Russian. Anything." I still couldn't get a fix on the frequency of her irony, if that was even the right word for it. Her self-consciousness was formless, sloshing over the meanings of her words and evaporating.

"I'm okay," I said.

"You don't drink?" she said.

"Not anymore," I said.

"Ah!" she said, and seized on the fact as her first major clue to my character. "You're an alcoholic. Well. We won't force you to drink, then. I don't want you to hit bottom! That's what you alcoholics do if you touch liquor, isn't it? You fall into a gutter and hit bottom? Well. I have milk. And soda pop. Just tell me. Whatever you like." Again, the sarcasm spilled over without object and disappeared as her attention flashed back to the fish. "I thought I'd put some rosemary on it. What do you think, Bobby? Should I? That's what the girls say to do."

"Sure." He was pouring his special bottle of porter into a giant stein with engraved decorations all over it. The handle and cap looked carved from ivory. The body seemed to include a stag in bas-relief. This was his special mug, I gathered, used only once a week to receive his special bottle of beer.

"These girls I know," Maggie said to me, "they know how to do everything. They grow special beans. Can you believe it? You go to their house and they're kneading homemade bread and washing their salad greens in fairy piss and eating strawberries that aren't strawberries but actually some ancestors of strawberries that grow on the mountains in Cameroon. They make their own plates for every meal. They spin them on a ceramics wheel. And they put their homemade beans in them. I hate eating, personally. I'd stop if I could. I just want to live on seeds and air."

"Good luck," Cave said from behind his stein. His whole demeanor had shifted in the presence of Maggie, his non-girlfriend. He'd become visibly more relaxed, even a sliver macho. He leaned against the counter, holding his beer stein in both hands, and watched Maggie with a barely suppressed affection. I saw the bond clearly for a moment. They loved each other, and this was how they whiled away the hours of their lives, cooking and drinking and talking about beans. These were the moments of Cave's life that would flow by unremembered, untouched by any ideology or regret. Watching them together, I didn't really have any questions. I only found I missed Sobie.

*   *   *

Maggie pulled the salmon with its beads of white fat from the oven and messily plated our meals. Then we carried our dinners back into the entertainment room to watch a basketball game. The basketball game was a weekly ritual, I learned, part of fish night. From a hall closet Cave pulled matching dinner trays and arranged them beside each other in front of the white couch. I was directed to sit on a recliner off to the side, with an end table for my water glass. When everyone was ensconced, Maggie located a remote and held it in front of her, pointing in the general direction of the screen, clicking randomly until she landed on the right channel.

"This is what he misses," Maggie said, as the cheering arena in Beijing appeared. "I could care less. I think soccer is fine. The men are all short here, so they play soccer. Basketball isn't the thing. I don't care."

"Fútbol," Cave corrected. "They call soccer fútbol here. Like everywhere. You should know that."

The Clippers were playing the Dragons tonight. Cave and Maggie weren't rooting for either team, as far as I could tell, but they seemed to know all the players and their season stats. They enjoyed impressing each other with their trivia. It was funny how they chose not to call themselves a couple when they were obviously such a couple. Did she know they weren't a couple? I wondered. Did he know they were? And did she know who he really was? It seemed impossible that she didn't know but also, possibly, not impossible. She might have yet to discover that her boyfriend's entire history previous to meeting her was a falsehood.

As in a certain kind of couple, it became Maggie's job to entertain me.

"What are you doing for the holidays?" she said. She was so bored by the question she could barely finish it, but she seemed to understand it was expected.

"Not really sure," I said. "I'll try to head home soon, most likely. There's a lot up in the air."

"Is there a lady friend at home?" she said. "Or maybe a man? Are you gay?"

"There might be a lady," I said. "It's too early to know. We'll see."

"Oh. What is she like?" Her interest ticked upward a degree in the vicinity of sex.

"I don't know exactly what it is yet."

"'What we cannot speak about, we must pass over in silence,'" she said. "That's Wittgenstein. The sage."

I raised my eyebrow and tapped my nose, making a show of not saying anything, and she smiled approvingly. Again, Maggie had surprised me, adding another facet. We went back to watching the game. The Dragons were in a scoring drought, unable to convert. The Clippers were hitting their threes. Maggie paid attention for a few plays, but soon enough she couldn't help herself and disobeyed her own tautological edict. "Would she come down here to live with you?"

"I doubt it," I said. "But we're a long way from that conversation."

She turned back to the game. I wasn't giving her anything interesting enough to merit further digging. Soon Cave got up and shuffled to the bathroom, leaving us alone, which made things all the more awkward. We were both satellites of Bob this evening, and without his gravity, we were prone to drift apart. The game was deep in the irrelevant plains of the second quarter, heading for a commercial break. Gradually, the lack of conversation started to seem pointed.

"What are you doing for the holidays?" I said.

"We have to go to Cabo," she said.

"That sounds nice," I said.

"No it doesn't," she said. "We have to take a boat because Bob won't fly. And we have to meet all his boring, fascist friends. Good lord, what a waste of time. Maybe I won't go. Cabo San Lucas. What a terrible place. Have you ever been?"

"I haven't," I said.

"It's like North Korea meets the Occupied Territories meets a Chili's restaurant," she said, finishing another drink. "Golf carts and disco music. It's like psychological torture. You go to the bar and the music is playing. You sit on the deck and the music is playing. You sit by the pool and the music is playing. But these friends of Bob's love it there. They are such assholes. They like to ride golf carts from the pool to the buffet table. I thought those resorts would disappear after the Upheavals, you know? But people like them, it turns out. They do! They like fake, plastic, sanitized experiences better than anything. They like to come all the way down from North America to take their picture with a palm tree and go inside and watch the same TV they'd watch at home. I swear."

"These are friends of his from the US you're meeting?" I said.

"No one lives in the US anymore," she said. "But they all grew up there. Bob went to college with one of them or something. I don't know."

"Does he have a lot of friends from those days?" I said.

"Aren't you nosy!" she said, but seemed pleased by my interest. "No. He barely keeps in touch with anyone. He's very picky that way. He's like a monk. You're lucky he chose you. It's very rare."

"I'm honored," I said.

"I'm always telling him," she said, " 'You should see more people! It's nice to meet people! Get out more! Travel!' But he always says he doesn't want to. He says he likes to travel 'in time instead of space.' He means reading books."

"That makes sense to me," I said.

"No wonder he likes you."

"Mag," Cave interrupted. He'd returned from the bathroom and was standing listening in the hall doorway. "Jake doesn't want to hear about that. It's boring."

"I'm just saying you should get out more," she said. "See how nice it is meeting a new person? You don't have to be such a hermit."

"I'm not a hermit," he said, retaking his seat. "I live in a city."

"You can be a hermit in a city," she said. "There are lots of them. You should enjoy yourself more, that's all."

"I'm enjoying myself right now," he said.

"New people bring new energy," she said. "I think Jake agrees with me. He wants to see you at a party sometime. Or maybe go to Paris with you. That's what Jake wants. Don't you, Jake? Anywhere but Cabo, my God."

"Maggie . . . ," Cave said.

"Cabo is terrible, Jake. Those people are such assholes. I have to complain."

"Please, Maggie . . ." Cave patted her on the leg, a signal of what I had no idea.

*   *   *

Fish night lasted exactly the duration of the basketball game. As soon as the buzzer sounded and the Clippers triumphed, we all rose and said good night. There was some talk about Cave spending the night, but the negotiation seemed mostly for show. Cave was tired, he said. He wanted to sleep in his own bed tonight.

"You should take a car," Maggie said.

"I'll walk," he said. "It's fine."

"You can't walk all the way," she said.

"I'll take the subway, then," he said.

"Jake, tell him to take a car," she said.

"I'm not getting involved," I said.

"Then you're the one to blame if anything happens."

I ended up walking him to the subway. It was on my route, anyway, and once we were outside, I saw he needed a little help navigating the evening crowds. We came to an easy, unspoken alliance at crosswalks and bottlenecks, with me drifting close to his side and wedging us through the bodies, keeping a hand close to his elbow just in case, and him pretending nothing was happening. Along the way, we talked about Maggie and how much he adored her.

"She's not like anyone I know," he said. "She's a bit wild, I know, but she has certain powers I can't really explain. She's in touch with certain currents of energy. She knows things that she shouldn't be able to know. She could've been an astrophysicist. Or a poet. I never liked regular people that much. And she's really not regular. What can I say?"

"You're lucky you found each other," I said.

"If we were younger, we'd be lucky," he said. "If we'd met each other at a different time, earlier in our lives, that would have been a very different story. But it's something anyway. It is what it is. Let's talk about something else. Are you looking at any houses this week?"

"Not sure," I said. "I'm taking my time."

"That's the way!" he said. "Take your time. What's the rush? Have you bribed anyone yet? That can help down here sometimes, you know."

"Not yet," I said. "Maybe I should."

"It isn't required," he said. "But it can be helpful. Ahh. I remember the first time I bribed a police officer. That was quite a day. I was only seventeen. I'd driven down to Mexico with a friend of mine in a beat-up old van. We had American plates, so we might as well have painted a target on the roof. Or a dollar sign. We got pulled over all the time, everywhere we went. In Guerrero, we ran out of money and had to pay the federales with a can of WD-40. It turned out they loved a can of WD-40. They lubed their rifles with it. We started carrying extra cans, just in case.

"Those were different times," he said, jostling his way toward the yellow light of the subway station. "If I'd known how dangerous that trip was, I never would've gone. Thank God I didn't know. I'm so glad I went."

At the subway entrance we stood and warmly shook hands.

"Thanks for everything," I said. "The cathedral. And dinner. All of it."

"I'm glad you enjoyed the murals," he said. "I thought you might. Orozco's up there with our friend Mr. Clemens, in my opinion. Maybe I'll see you at the café soon. After the holidays."

"So you're leaving soon?" I said.

"Tomorrow," he said. "We'll be gone for a couple weeks. Maggie complains about it, but she loves the beach."

"Then I'll see you when you get back," I said. "At the museum."

"Hasta luego," he said.

And I watched him as he descended the stairs into the earth.

8

The Dallas/Fort Worth International Airport was a palace of plastic and Teflon. The people-mover's treadmill rolled through the endless, air-conditioned concourse; the food courts sprawled over vast floors of gleaming vinyl; the glass atria soared, filled with colorful aluminum mobiles. And somewhere inside the walls, enmeshed in the architecture, the biometric scanners recorded every passenger's vocal intonation, blinking pattern, mouth shape, and body temperature, assessing national identities and levels of threat. They must have judged mine acceptable because every door I approached opened, every siren remained silent. By the time I reached my gate, I'd been fully vetted. I was back in the USA.

I arrived back in town close to midnight and took a cab straight to Liu's house, scene of the *Constant Globe*'s annual holiday party. It was the same party every year, Aliyah told me, a seasonal display of Liu's soft power, with a guest list including his staff and their partners, his political friends, and select figures from the city's self-appointed social elite. There were always martinis and mushroom-based canapés served, poinsettias on every surface, a DJ related to one of the guests. Everyone in the office complained about it, she said, and yet they always ended up staying too late.

By the time I arrived, the party was spilling out onto the deck of Liu's riverside mansion, guests babbling and laughing over the moonlit waters. I found Liu slumped in a deck chair under an outdoor heater lamp. I could tell he'd been drinking because his shirt was misbuttoned and he had wet cheese on his fingers. As soon as he saw me, he hauled himself upright, grinning, wiping his hands, and for a second it almost seemed like he was going to hug me, but he started patting me on the back instead. When his mood was high, there was no hiding his innate affection for the people in his employ.

"You're here," he said. "Great, great. How was the flight?"

"It was fine," I said. "I—"

"No, wait," he said. "Don't tell me anything yet. Let's find Aliyah and go somewhere quiet. Come with me. Come, come . . ."

He took my arm and guided me through the crowd, knocking into wineglasses and smoldering cigars without apology. We found Aliyah near the buffet table talking to the copy editor, and Liu went over and grabbed her without any explanation. From there, he led us side by side out of the dining room, through the kitchen, down a hall, and into his home office, a private, book-lined sanctuary muffled from the party's noise. Aliyah and I took seats on the overstuffed leather couches, and Liu sat at his giant, cluttered desk. We'd exited *Gatsby* world and entered Liu's *Godfather* fantasy, three schemers in a hushed, oak-paneled room.

"You're back," Liu said, clapping his palms to commence our meeting. "Guadalajara. So!" He giggled and drummed his fingers on the desk. I got the sense he was trying to express his pleasure and possibly even pay me a compliment, but with Liu nothing ever came out straight. The best he could do was shake his head and chuckle some more while rifling through his drawers.

"Amazing work," Aliyah said. "I don't know how you got in there so fast."

"It was the book," I said. "The book opened the door."

"The book opened the door, maybe," she said. "But you walked through it, all the way into his girlfriend's apartment. Jesus. We have enough footage and audio for a documentary now."

"Two documentaries!" Liu said. "And extras for the deep-access subscribers."

"And raw data for the sustaining circle," Aliyah said. "It'll keep us going a long time, Jack. It's great."

"I'm glad the footage looks okay," I said. "I wasn't sure how it would read to someone who wasn't in the rooms."

"We can stabilize the rougher stuff," she said. "And we can clean up the sound. All we need now is archival footage and expert testimony and we'll be ready for the Donaldson."

"The what?" Liu said.

It seemed Aliyah hadn't told Liu about the Donaldson. "The Donaldson" was our shorthand for the final interview with Cave, the ultimate, recorded confession or denial, either one, it didn't matter which. To Aliyah and me, the Donaldson was the self-evident end point of our whole project, but to Liu, it turned out, it wasn't so self-evident at all.

"But we already have everything we need," Liu said. "The data points are irrefutable."

"We need Cave's reaction, Liu," Aliyah said. "It's part of the structure of this kind of thing. It's how this kind of piece works."

"But we know who he is!" Liu said. "It doesn't matter what he says anymore! We've got him!"

They went back and forth on the subject, arguing like siblings. Liu wanted to get the story out as quickly as possible. The competition was probably right behind us, he said. He was willing to cut corners if it meant being first. Aliyah, for her part, wanted to wait. The Donaldson was the payoff of the whole thing, she argued. The audience had to know that Cave knew what was happening to him. They wanted to see the investigation come to its final reveal. They wanted me and Cave in the same frame together. That was what they watched this kind of thing for, the drama.

It took Liu some time to comprehend what Aliyah was saying. As a deeply metric-based person, he often missed the finer nuances of storytelling. Although the outcome of the argument was never really in question, it went on for a long time, mostly so Liu could come to his defeat with some level of dignity.

"It won't take much longer, Liu," Aliyah said. "I already have the names of a few cameramen we might want to use. I'll be getting clips from them starting tomorrow. I have someone doing archival searches and organizing those files. The talking-head interviews we could have shot by New Year's. We should be ready as soon as Cave gets back from Cabo. We just have to do this right."

Liu never explicitly capitulated, but eventually the argument petered out and we returned to our original, shared enthusiasm. There were so many tactics to discuss, so many logistics to figure out. It was fun. We talked about the geography of Guadalajara, the art displayed on Maggie's walls. We could have kept scheming away for hours, but the party was still happening beyond the walls of Liu's home office, and our absence was likely becoming noticeable. Finally, with regret, we ended the session, congregating at the door for one more round of mutual congratulations.

"Fantastic work, Jack," Liu said, putting his hand on my shoulder with rare fatherly warmth. "You really got him. This is a big deal. Really big deal."

"You nailed him, all right," Aliyah said. "He's got no idea what's coming at him."

"No, he definitely does not," I said, and, with a small twinge of remorse, followed them out the door, back into the party's golden world of music and laughter.

*　　*　　*

It was a beautiful thing to sleep in my own bed again, unbothered by air fresheners or backfiring engines. I slept in a state of dreamless oblivion, like I was buried in mud. In the morning I got up and dealt with the bureaucracy of my life. I paid my bills, paid my rent, and sorted the junk mail.

I called my mom in Ohio for our seasonal catch-up, hearing all about her winter dahlias, which were still blooming because there'd been no frost this year. She'd have them all the way into spring if the weather kept up, she said, making no connection between the dahlias in December and the flooding in April or the fires in June or the mega thaw a thousand miles to the north. Afterward, I fixed my kitchen sink. I replaced the old seat and springs and reinserted the ball assembly, and when I turned the water on and off the leaking had stopped. Voilà. Why hadn't I done that long ago?

The rest of the morning I spent Christmas shopping. This year the trends in the boutiques near my apartment were cubes of French soap, hammered-tin necklaces, and air plants from Peru, nothing anyone I knew wanted or needed. But the expedition didn't end up a total loss. During my rounds, I managed to return a few calls, leaving messages for Jeff Catalog, postponing a future lunch; my tax lady, promising the signatures she wanted; and Dr. Breeze, who'd been calling for some kind of post-examination interview. Again, the balls were back in their courts, and I was free.

I would have kept shopping, but I had a date with Sobie that night. She said she wanted to eat dinner at my place rather than go out, which meant a thorough scrubbing was in order. I went home and vacuumed, mopped, laundered the bedsheets and bathroom towels, and spent a long time just drifting from room to room, shifting objects from one place to another. I fell into a kind of trance, cleaning without any method, and in the end, although the apartment didn't look much different than before, I felt like the space was somehow renewed.

I showered. I shaved. I put on a fresh, pale blue oxford. Then I pulled together the ingredients for a Spanish tortilla with spinach and feta. As I grilled the onions, the apartment filled with their sweet, caramelized smell. My place started to seem almost homey.

Sobie arrived not long after eight. She came in on a cold current of air, the winter chill blowing through the door and giving her cheeks a high glow. Her eyes were full of winter sparks, too, quick flashes from the wry, black depths. She hurried inside and shrugged off her coat to reveal a silky, sleeveless dress underneath. The pattern was orange squibs on a yellow background, a shot of summer, and the staticky fabric clung to her skin. She had to peel it from her hips and thighs, rubbing away the charge, letting the dress fall to its proper drape.

"Parking in your neighborhood really sucks," she said. "I had to park five blocks away. And it's so cold and wet out there! Why do we live here, anyway?"

"It's really bad out there, I know," I said. "It keeps getting worse. The parking, I mean."

"People in this town need to figure out how to park closer together," she said. "It's not that hard. The city should make everyone take a seminar or something. 'Here's how you park, you stupid idiot. You don't need to leave half a car length on both sides.'" Her voice, with its low, amused timbre, made the complaints almost the opposite of complaints. "Not that you care," she said. "You had sun this week. You look like you've been lying around by a pool."

"Not exactly," I said. "But vitamin D, yeah."

Sobie placed her big shoulder bag on the back of the couch and started digging around inside, throwing her compact and loose dollar bills on the dining room table. She said she'd brought me something, an early holiday present, and withdrew a shiny, beribboned package. She tossed it over. It was something squishy, like a T-shirt.

"Let's do presents now," she said.

"Already?" I said.

"I'm not into waiting," she said. "Are you?"

I was happy to be commanded by her. Thankfully I had a present ready myself, something I'd picked up in Mexico. We sat on the yellow couch and set our gifts next to each other on the coffee table. She waited while I opened mine first. I took my time inspecting her handmade holiday card, a scrap of heavy construction paper with a collage of flower prints cut from magazines, nothing genius, but an effort. "With affection," the card read. I pretended it was remarkable but not too remarkable. I didn't want to go overboard. Then I untied the fat string around the package and opened the gift in a mild frenzy. Inside the wrapping paper was a blue wool scarf with red patches, something like stripes, but tortured. One end was much wider than the other, and the purling varied greatly. It looked more like the reflection of a scarf in a rippling pond than an actual scarf.

"It's my first one," she said. "I'm just starting to knit."

"I love it," I said.

The present I gave her was a book of dog photographs. I'd thought it would read as an expression of friendship, fidelity, something like that, but watching her flip through the glossy pages, I could see the book wasn't what I'd imagined. These dogs were poor. They were mostly living in rural Mexico, tied to starving trees in barren dirt yards. They seemed like they'd been bred to fight. I hadn't looked closely enough. I'd bought her a photo book of Mexican fighting dogs.

"I don't know what I was thinking," I said. "This is a terrible book. I'll take it back."

"No, no," she said, pulling it away. "I'll just put it on a high shelf so my daughter won't see it. But I want it. It's great."

She placed the book out of my reach and turned and leaned over to give me a thank-you hug. I leaned in to hug her, too. The hug went on longer than strictly necessary. I smelled her clean hair near my face, felt her soft heat through her silken dress. When she finally pulled away, she didn't return all the way to an upright position, but hovered closely in front of me. I almost had no choice but to lean in and kiss her. Our lips touched. The night was unfolding much more quickly than I'd expected.

I pulled away and looked into her black eyes again. The blackness was gleaming, alive with daring. We laughed and went in and kissed again.

"Are you hungry?" I said.

"I'm actually not that hungry," she said.

"That's fine," I said. "It'll keep. No problem."

"Good," she said.

A few minutes later we got up from the couch and stumbled into the bedroom. We weren't nervous or confused anymore. We weren't waiting for anything to begin or end. Sobie refused to listen to any apologies about my hairy physique or my ugly sleeping quarters. She told me to just shut up and lie down, this was happening.

*   *   *

Afterward, we lay side by side, speaking quietly about nothing much. Regarding the larger questions about what we were doing, or what we wanted this to be, or where we thought this might be going, we stayed quiet. We didn't feel the need to talk about the good luck that'd led us to this place, or the clues that had been planted long ago. We didn't have to postulate about whether we would've been ready then, or if we'd been too young, or if on some level we'd known that we'd have this other chance. We didn't need to define anything. We didn't need to address the implications, not yet.

Instead, we played dumb games with our fingers and gossiped about her friends who might become my friends again as the rain thrummed on the eaves, pouring off the roof, finishing in a low, moaning spatter on the wet ground. The old gutters of the pre-century buildings weren't made for this volume of tropical downpour. The deluges overpowered the whole city.

I massaged her back for a long time, learning the good spots up and down her spine.

"Maybe I'll have to come down and visit you in Mexico if I need a back rub," she said.

"You should," I said, thumbing a nerve cluster at the base of her neck. I widened my fingers, raking her back.

"How long will you be down there, anyway?" she said.

"Hard to say," I said. "Probably not that long."

I made my hand into a basket and dragged it through her hair, kneading her scalp, eliciting sounds of approval.

"Are you gonna bust him?" she said.

"That's the plan," I said.

"Is it going to be dangerous?" she said.

"No," I said. "He's almost eighty years old."

"Careful. He might gum you to death."

"I should be careful," I said. "I might need to get some anti-gumming technology. I'll talk to the guys in the lab about that."

"Come here and gum me."

We ate in bed. She liked the Spanish tortilla. It wasn't too wet or too dry. We didn't watch anything on my monitor because we'd already pulled everything we wanted with us into this room; we didn't need anything else. She fell asleep soon after the brownies I'd made for dessert. She warned me she was a great sleeper, and it was true, she started snoring within moments. I lay awake, listening to the rain. It whispered and coughed, spattering against the windows, driven by the fitful wind. Finally the rain stopped and moonlight welled in the curtains, and I went to the window to see the moon but I couldn't find it. Just a strip of black sky where moon-burned clouds were ripping apart in a high wind.

I walked out to the front porch for a better view. The street was a lake of rainwater, shimmering under the lamplight. Low clouds coursed into nothingness, twisting into vapor and disappearing. I stood on the porch in my robe, watching the show, letting my body's heat drift away. I kept standing there until the cold started invading my pores and then my bones. I waited until my teeth were almost chattering, and the sky was perfectly clear. Moonlight poured down through the void. Finally, freezing, I went back inside and joined Sobie's heat in the bed.

*　　*　　*

Sobie left in the morning, and there was nothing weird or forced about it. She seemed happy she'd come, and thus I was happy she'd been there. We knew we wouldn't be seeing each other for a while, as she and her daughter had a busy week ahead, but that was fine, too. We'd crossed into something, and now whatever came next could wait.

I decided to drive to the outlet stores and deal with my Christmas shopping. I could usually find something for my cousins and their kids out there, boring, midwestern, brand-forward articles they could've bought for themselves at their own outlet malls. In a rented flex car, with a giant cup of coffee in hand, I headed off into the winter light. Coffee, velocity, music, fresh memories of Sobie's body in my mind: How much pleasure could a single morning contain?

The drive was forty-five minutes straight south. The freeway was wet from the late-night showers, a shifting palette of silver and pearl. The crummy buildings at the city's edge ended after twenty minutes, giving way to wheat fields and a long view of the coastal mountains to the west, their dark flanks streaked with brushstrokes of mist. The sky was pallid, with charcoal details. I had a few calls to return along the way, the messages having returned to my in-box, and I made them one by one, checking them off my list. I talked to the tax lady and made some promises about the paperwork I owed her. I talked to Jeff, telling him nothing very specific. I also reached Dr. Breeze's office, expecting to leave another message, but this time he happened to be near the phone. The nurse handed him the receiver.

"Sorry for taking a while," I said. "I've been out of the country the last week or so."

"That's okay," he said. "I'm glad you're calling now. I was going to call you again soon. I have something to tell you. I wonder if you're sitting down right now?"

"I'm in a car," I said.

"Okay," he said. "You might want to pull over for this."

With these words, my fingers and chest began to tingle. I hadn't noticed anything worrisome in the messages he'd been leaving, they'd been businesslike but not dire-sounding. If I was supposed to sit down, though, what did that mean? The fields and mountains seemed to recede, making room for whatever was about to fall.

"I think I'm okay here," I said. The road ahead was clear and straight. I could hold my path, whatever words came into my ear.

"Well, when you were here last," he said, "and we tested your eyes, we discovered the growths in your irises, the prions."

"I remember," I said.

"The prions," he said, "like I said, can be indicative of certain conditions. I had the data interpreted by the lab. I don't think we were totally accurate in assessing the risk before. I'm sorry about that. I should have been more cautious. Like I said, the prions are not themselves malignant, but they can foretell a malignancy.

I think I gave the chances at the time as 'one in a million,' but that isn't really correct. From what I'm seeing now, you're more exposed to risk than I thought."

"Okay," I said. "Like, how much?"

"There are so many variables involved," he said. "It isn't anything we can quantify precisely."

"Do you have a best guess?" I said.

"It wouldn't really mean anything," he said. "It would be more speculation on my part. At best."

"A ballpark?" I said. The reporter in me intuitively grasped for a fact. I wanted a number again. Something I could use.

"I'd rather not," he said.

"I understand it's only an opinion," I said. "I'd still like to know."

"If I had to say something," he said, "I'd say more like one in ten. If I had to say."

The car continued zooming onward. Nothing inside or outside of the car had physically changed, but everything surrounding me had become heavy and thick.

"Have you been showing any symptoms since I saw you?" he said. "Memory issues, fever, balance issues, mood issues?"

"I don't think so," I said.

"Any emotional swings? Visual oddities?"

"No."

"Okay. Those are good signs. Or rather, they aren't bad signs."

"Is there more testing I need to do?" I said, which seemed like the right question to ask. "I'm going out of town again soon. I'm not sure how long I'll be gone."

"That's optional," he said. "You could come and see me if you wanted to. We could measure the development of the prions and see if there's been any advancement in the growth. But I don't know if I'd recommend that or not."

That was when I realized I was doomed. Dr. Breeze was advising me to stop seeking any further information. He was saying, without openly saying it, that the one-in-ten ratio he was talking about was only a mirage. He was telling me, in so many words, there was no reason to hope. Because he was a decent, professional person, he was breaking the news to me gently. He was delivering a death sentence but leaving a crack in the door just in case.

I drove onward, although the road had disappeared. The wheels seemed to float in gray space.

"What kind of time frame are we talking about here?" I heard myself ask. "Worst case."

"Impossible to say," he said. "But once the symptoms begin, things move fairly quickly. But if they don't present, nothing happens. We just don't know."

"Okay."

"Do you have a therapist?" he said. "Or a counselor of any kind? Someone to talk to? This can be a stressful position to be in, I know . . ." His voice was starting to disintegrate, lost inside the rising silence in my brain, the teeming static that was swallowing all.

I must have asked questions because he continued talking. From what I could understand, his new thinking mostly derived from a medical paper he'd dug up from 2034. The paper had compared the progression of Creutzfeldt–Jakob disease—one of the forms my diagnosis could take—to that of scrapie in sheep and goats, chronic wasting disease in deer and elk, and kuru among cannibals. The researchers had built a model displaying the conversion rate among members of those groups from initial infection to full-blown disease, and the model suggested a rate higher than Dr. Breeze had initially assumed. That was where his one-in-ten number came from, but that ratio, he stressed, was only a guess. The studies had ended with the animal testing ban of 2037, so the data sets were limited.

There was also the question of the incubation period, he said.

"No one really knows how or when the autocatalytic process is initiated," his voice said. "Some researchers find the mere idea of a protein devoid of nucleic acid that can dictate its own replication heretical. That said, there are some theories that suggest the likelihood might increase with age, in which case, it might be beneficial to measure how long the prions have already existed in your irises. There are some tests we could run and specialists to consult, if you really want to go that path."

"What kind of tests are we talking about?" I said.

"One is called an olfactoral neuron scrape," he said. "It involves inserting a fiber-optic rhinoscope into your nasal cavity, along with a sterile brush, and kind of rolling it along the mucosal surface to collect neurons. It isn't very pleasant. There's also something called a 'real-time quaking-induced conversion.' That one isn't pleasant, either. Those are the main ones."

"Do you think I should do them?" I said.

"I don't think you need to do anything right now," he said. "Neither of those tests are great indicators of anything, from what I understand. And since there's no treatment for the disease, anyway, I still don't see the point. So we're back where we were before."

By the time we hung up, the world outside didn't exist. All my senses were on my skin. I couldn't feel the prions inside me, but I imagined them as microscopic maggots squirming down in the molecular depths. How very strange, I thought, to be smited on the way to the outlet mall. Here I'd been thinking death was so far away, all the way on the other side of the globe, loitering in a meadow or buying some iced tea. But he'd been standing beside me the whole time.

The song on the radio was an oldie. It was a soul song from the 1960s, one I'd always liked. It summoned nostalgia for a time long before I'd even existed. The singer's voice was so real, it felt like she was in the car with me. I could see the light in the room where she'd recorded the album, that beautiful overcast light coating the houseplants. Maybe it was a record cover I was thinking of. I allowed myself to fall into the song, letting the notes have their way. I wasn't going to die in the next three minutes, so I could enjoy myself for that long at least. The view outside the windshield was dun and gray. How softly and suddenly I'd crossed this meridian.

I took the exit and pulled into the parking lot. I found a space not far from the entrance to the Adidas store. I sat there for a moment, wondering if I should drive home, but I still had errands to do; nothing had altered that fact. I got out of the car and walked alongside an empty field where hardy grass and weeds riddled the poor earth. The smallest wind shook the tiny stalks of grass. The blades shivered. Here was more life, growing in its most humble formation. I was seeing the whole, fragile world through the growing prions.

I went inside the Old Navy store and browsed the racks like always. Everything had changed, and yet no one in the world knew anything about it, only me. I moved through the aisles at half-speed, drifting from island to island. The smell of the new fabric was almost overpowering. The detergents left a thin residue on my fingers as I pushed the garments back and forth. The sound of the ceramic hangers was reassuring. My whole life I'd heard that sound. I had memories of my mother shifting the hangers while I hid in the racks. Maybe if I kept shifting I'd spot myself in there.

Soon I found an acceptable sweater for my mom. It was a blue sweater with a green crest on the chest. I found some windbreakers for my cousins. Red, green, and gray, one for each. And I bought myself some socks with the thick sponge I liked. How strange, I thought, carrying the clothes to the register, to think these good socks rolling on the conveyer belt might outlast me. And how nice that my shopping was already done.

9

I flew back to Guadalajara on New Year's Day, 2052. The last week of the year had been blissfully dull and free of any physical symptoms listed in the journals. No ataxia, no spasticity, no akinetic mutism. Deboarding, I felt clean, and the city felt clean, too, like a hard wind had blown through, sweeping the holiday decorations off the walls and the trash from the ground, leaving the surfaces blank. Quietly, coldly, we'd crossed into the new year.

I had a better hotel room at the Best Western this time around. Liu seemed to smell some kind of glory down in Mexico, and he'd placed the resources not only of the newspaper's travel budget but of some of his personal bank account behind me. The new room was a suite on the twelfth floor, with windows that opened and a little kitchenette with a stovetop and mini-fridge. I could see the rooftops sprawling in every direction, decorated with clotheslines and satellite dishes and bursts of palm trees, and faraway the tips of ancient, surrounding hills. When I checked in, a breeze was gently blowing through, scented with cement dust and frijoles. It was good to be Liu's chosen emissary, I thought. If I had to carve his name in the annals of history with my flaming sword to get this upgrade, so be it.

I took a nap. The mattress was too soft, and the traffic horns blared on and off at irregular intervals. I couldn't fall asleep, so I ended up spending hours staring at the ceiling, testing my brain in light of my recent diagnosis. I'd been making a conscious effort to dredge up old memories, seeking the limits of my mental powers. I went through every member of my grade school soccer team. I recollected the smell of my friend Josh's Toyota Corolla. I walked the banks of the nameless creek running through my hometown where as kids we used to hunt crawdads and, later, smoked our first cigarettes. I roamed every year, every season, picking up impressions and checking them for damage.

Had anything been lost? I wondered. I didn't think so. I still seemed to have all the images and facts I'd had before, such as they were. I still couldn't sleep, so I sat on the bed and tried staring hard at the furniture in the room, zooming in on the doorknob and the lampshade, trying to feel the prions physically replicating in my eyes. I couldn't sense anything in that way, either. I didn't know what a misfolded protein felt like. I didn't know what a neuron felt like, or an enzyme, or a cytoplasm. They were all just words. My breathing seemed normal. My muscles and nerves responded to orders.

I must have slept, because I woke up to the sound of birdcalls. They weren't birds I recognized, but for a moment I imagined I was in my childhood bed. I'd grown up hearing orioles and chickadees, as I recalled, but at some point they'd all moved north, replaced by more southerly finches and warblers. Happily, the birds I heard now, in Mexico, were beautiful singers, too.

*   *   *

Toward evening, I went to buy some groceries and found new things afoot in the city—or one new thing, anyway. I'd been gone only two weeks, and a raft of new posters had already been plastered onto the buses and construction site fences. I didn't understand what they were advertising at first, only that they were big and ubiquitous, rows of wheat-pasted multiples sporting striated orange-and-purple backgrounds, with black sunbeams radiating through white text. The text said something about group tours and hotel deals, as far as I could tell, but the fuller meaning was a puzzle.

I noticed street vendors hawking branded T-shirts and mugs with a similar orange-and-purple color scheme. And standing in line at the grocery store with my eggs and toast and coffee, I saw the same color scheme yet again, this time on a rack of disposable sunglasses. The glasses were flimsy cardboard frames with plastic, polarized lenses glued on the face side. I finally got it. An eclipse was coming.

The cashier spoke some English and explained this wasn't just a normal eclipse, either. This was a full solar eclipse, or what they called the Totality. Every few years, the path of Totality swept across a lucky swath of the globe, and for between a few seconds and about six and a half minutes, the moon completely blotted the sun from view. This year, she explained, the Totality crossed Mexico, and millions of eclipse tourists were even now streaming into the country to watch. They'd be setting up camping chairs in empty fields and rolling out towels on the beaches, waiting for the shadow to fall. And where there were solar tourists arriving from around the world, she said, there were entrepreneurs to profit off their needs and pleasures. I passed on the glasses, but I thanked her for the information.

Back at the hotel I called Aliyah, who was almost finished assembling the background materials. She'd be done very soon, she said, at which point we'd be ready to move on to the Donaldson. Until then, I should just keep watch over Cave, making sure he didn't leave town or do anything bizarre.

"So don't make any contact," I said, confirming my orders.

"We don't want to make him suspicious at all," she said. "Don't you think?"

"But I should keep an eye on him," I said.

"Just keep tabs on him," she said. "Use your own judgment. I trust you to do what's best." By which she meant she didn't entirely trust me. Which was fine. I didn't exactly trust myself.

I began the surveillance the next morning, seated on a bench across from the museum. From my new seat I could see my old café window, uninhabited, and I could see the front entrance, sporadically sucking in and spitting out visitors. I was far enough away that no one could sense me as they approached but close enough that I could easily identify Cave. I sat and waited. Cars and buses passed by silently, emblazoned with eclipse ads. Pedestrians clustered and dispersed in the courtyard, crossing the long shadow of the sculpture of Hidalgo. At around 11:00 a.m., Cave showed up, shuffling across the flagstones and into the front door with a wave of his membership card. I knew he'd be in there for a few hours now.

Cars whirred. Clouds crept. I scratched at a rash that had appeared on my thigh a few days before, trying not to worry. Rashes weren't a listed symptom of my possible condition, but I was tempted to call Dr. Breeze anyway. I held back, though, not wanting to seem paranoid. I already knew what he'd say: It was nothing. We knew nothing. I put the rash out of my mind and watched the museum and breathed deeply, testing my lungs, testing my bones. I looked back at the front door. The itch yapped at me, and I scratched it.

I called Sobie for some distraction.

"I saw a dog riding the train today," she told me.

"Just a dog?" I said.

"Yeah, just a dog," she said. "All alone. It was pretty weird."

That did seem weird, I said. Like so many images confronting me lately, this one seemed to carry some kind of personal allegorical weight. A dog, riding a train, uncomprehending of the massive infrastructure bringing it to its destination. I was like that dog. And how odd that the image was appearing in my mind here, now, two thousand miles from the place where it was witnessed, carried into my imagination on the wavelengths of Sobie's amused, smoky voice. Two brains, bound by language, discussing a wayward dog. This was the kind of lightness I was living in, awed by everything.

I asked her to tell me more about her day, and she told me she'd had falafel for lunch and she'd decided not to buy some boots because of the dumb-looking fake fur on the cuff. I enjoyed hearing about her day. This was the level of reality where the mind could rest. She told me about a client who'd met a movie star at a baseball game and who'd embarrassed herself by telling him about her ten-year-old son's screenplay. And another client who was getting facial surgery at age thirty-five. Start early, he advised. The face starts to fall and there's no going back. He had no shame about it at all. We decided we greatly admired him.

I sat there on the bench, watching the museum door, listening to Sobie's lovely voice in my ear. She could have been reading me the directions on a frozen pizza box for all I cared. I was sorry to leave her when Cave came out and I had to follow.

"Adiós," I said.

"Good luck."

He exited wearing his camel coat, with a fedora and what looked like leather gloves. He tugged at the gloves as he walked briskly along the museum's southern wall, passing in front of me on the other side of the four-lane street and continuing on toward the neighborhood of Oblatos.

I crossed over to his side of the street and followed at a far remove, careful to keep a handful of bodies between us. Cave was tall and had a distinctive, partly folded-over, geriatric lope. He also walked quite slowly, so he was hard to lose. Along the way we ambled past a woman eating a crumbling pastry outside a panadería; two little brothers laughing in a dark window; a dog with perfect gray spots. It was the best kind of chase in my opinion, unhurried but mildly suspenseful. It was almost like golf, but without any of the petty scorekeeping. It was the mission I'd always dreamed of, just pure, mobilized watching, drawn along by another person's will and all the while perceiving, always perceiving.

Cave turned left, and I hurried to close the distance, catching sight of him just as he disappeared around the next corner. I made it to that corner just before he disappeared again, not all the way onto the next street this time, but much closer. He was climbing the steps into a long, low brick building fronted by some withered topiary and beds of dusty red gravel.

I paused on the corner. The street was narrow and didn't offer any great options for escape. If Cave came back out, I'd be caught in the open. I spent a few seconds gauging the exit routes and decided to risk a quick trip to a window just for a peek. The windows were filmy and high. I could see sloppily painted posters on the walls and laminated pages tacked to a corkboard, with bright letters that looked like handwriting samples. An elementary school.

I hustled away and found a hiding place at the end of the block, in the crosscurrent of some pleasant city smells: sugared bread from a bakery, tobacco smoke, and fresh masa heating on a griddle. I would've stayed on that corner all day, smelling the smells, watching the light shift on a distant wire fence, but Cave reappeared in a matter of minutes. He wasn't alone this time, but walking alongside a whole gaggle of schoolchildren. The kids walked in a ragged double line, chattering and laughing, and Cave walked close to the front, mostly talking to a little girl with a green ribbon in her hair. There was also a teacher and a teacher's aide, I guessed. They were going on a field trip.

I shadowed the class for three blocks until they stopped at a cathedral. The cathedral was old and Gothic, set back from the street with a scant little courtyard. The facade was grimy and time-softened like so much in Guadalajara. I watched as the kids formed a semicircle around Cave and listened to him deliver an extended lesson. I watched him pointing to the angelic figures in the archivolt and the frieze on the lintel, gently unpacking the meanings of the building's iconology and architecture. I couldn't hear what he said, but as he pointed to each embedded sculpture and offered a brief interpretation, the kids seemed rapt. How many generations of knowledge had been passed down in this stone? I wondered. Cave might have been among the few left who could coax the lessons out.

The kids asked a few questions and Cave answered them seriously and sometimes playfully. He got some laughs. He seemed to know the kids' names, and they seemed to know him, which led me to deduce he was a regular guest. He'd spent his life despoiling the earth, destroying these children's very future, and now he was giving them this gift of his knowledge. Although one could also say he was taking a gift from them, feeding on their innocent love and attention, finding undeserved absolution in their adoring gazes. He was like a person who'd given up meat late in life, only to pretend none of it had ever passed his lips. What a lucky guy, to avoid the consequences for so long. How Catholic.

After the lesson, the kids ate their lunches in the courtyard and Cave talked to the pretty young teacher, another undeserved intimacy. When the class adjourned, Cave stayed behind, waving goodbye, smiling affectionately. He adjusted his hat and the sun struck his face. He walked on.

I followed him to a grocery store. It was a fancy grocery store, with beautiful organic inventory. I watched him through the large plate glass windows, tracking him by his hat until he submerged into the remote shadows of the store's depths. Soon he surfaced from the teeming reflections and approached the cashier with his collected items. I watched him staring at his products on the counter as they rolled to the cashier and she rang them up. He waited until the very last moment to thank her with a quick smile.

He exited carrying a canvas bag, and I let him gain a few lengths on the sidewalk before starting after. He cut through a park, passing kids on the jungle gym, some soccer players, and some shoeless, sleeping men. He took his time skirting the central fountain, lingering to watch the water splashing into the basin. He seemed to enter a brief trance, staring at the calm ripples. Maybe he was reflecting on his years in Mauritania and Zanzibar, extracting nickel and copper for NovaChem's energy-conversion devices division. Or the years he'd spent in Brazil, overseeing the razing of humid tropical forest environments in search of deep-lodged pockets of natural gas. No one in the park ever would have guessed he was a killer of species, grappling with the anguish of a long career of despoliation. If in fact that was what he was doing. He might've been thinking of nothing at all.

He left the park, and soon we were turning onto his street. I was surprised we'd arrived there so quickly. I hadn't realized we were so close, and I felt two large chunks of the city's geography knitting together in my mind, the surrounding neighborhoods coalescing into a single map. After all these years, the shape of the world was still filling out for me, the colors still shading in.

I watched Cave from the corner as he walked his block and paused at a gate. He entered. The street was empty. I waited five minutes and strolled past his address, giving a quick glance at his building, the one I'd suspected all along. His address was 4356 Calle Ontario. Now I knew.

*   *   *

I called Sobie again that night, lying on the bed. She caught me up on the hours since we'd last talked. She'd been to the bank and the post office, she said, where she'd watched a guy picking his nose for five entire minutes without stopping, and later her daughter had thrown a tantrum about busing her plate that involved the words *fuck* and *craphole*. The big news, though, was about her neighbor, who'd been having a mystery affair for the past four months. Every few days, the neighbor had been having incredibly raucous sex, and Sobie hadn't been able to figure out who the partner was. Late at night, sometimes in the afternoon, the noises would start. The action was borderline violent. They sounded like crazed horses. What were they doing over there? Now, she said, at last, she knew who the neighbor was entertaining.

"It's his landlord," she said, delighted. "I heard them this afternoon, and then I saw her leaving a few minutes after. Mystery solved."

"Does he get a break on the rent?" I said.

"That's a very good question," she said. "I'll have to do some surveillance myself."

I could hear her fussing with the dishes as I told her about my own day, the low-intensity chase and the proliferating branding of the coming eclipse. There were now multiple T-shirt designs and competing disposable sunglasses flooding the stores. The solar tourists were starting to arrive in large numbers, recognizable by their camera cases and elaborate, wide-brimmed hats. I could hear plates and silverware jostling in the sink. We seemed to be floating in some bodiless limbo.

"My mom saw the Totality in 2017," Sobie said. "She told me I should never miss it if I had a chance."

"It's not too late," I said. "You should come down."

"I couldn't get the time off," she said. "I wish."

"It doesn't happen very often," I said. "Might be worth it."

"You don't have time, either," she said. "I don't want to see it alone."

I pushed her a little longer, urging her to take the opportunity and come to Mexico. I pushed harder than I might have, mainly because I knew she never would. And then, with great sweetness, we said good night.

*　　*　　*

Two days later, I woke up early in the morning with a faint ache in my temples. I didn't like having a headache, even a small, insignificant headache like this one, and I lay in bed for a few minutes gauging my body's equilibrium. I sent sensors into my fingers, into my lungs. I tried to feel my nerve endings and my endocrine system. I wasn't registering any listed symptoms, but by now the scanning had become almost continuous. A day ago I'd noticed clouds in my vision and I'd almost broken down before realizing it was just that my glasses were dirty. In the afternoon, I'd experienced a spell of light-headedness, but a torta had fixed that. For a week, at least, in addition to the rash on my thigh, I'd been feeling the scratch of a sore throat near my tonsils, but it always disappeared before I could pin it down, a mere phantom. The machinery of my body was running fine, but under everything I couldn't help sensing the folding, mutating prions and their dupes.

I made coffee and started the morning on Cave's block. Knowing his address, I didn't need to intercept him at the museum anymore, I could just start at the origin. I got there early, found a hidden alcove, and watched.

He emerged midmorning, carrying a backpack. I assumed he was going to the museum as usual, but instead he bent off course and walked north. We crossed over a pedestrian bridge and alongside a train yard, strolling slowly into a light industrial section of the city I'd never visited before. The buildings were old and ramshackle, with dilapidated loading bays and masses of graffiti on every wall up to arm-reach level, the immortal Wild Style of the late-twentieth-century Bronx. The roads were heavily potholed, with start-and-stop railroad tracks sunk in the macadam, and among the signs we passed were ones advertising a paint factory, a produce distributor, and an office supply warehouse. I had to keep far back because the streets were almost deserted and Cave was incredibly slow.

Today's destination was a four-story building encrusted with fire escapes. The ground floor was divided between a furniture store and a printing shop, but Cave didn't go into either of those places. He walked around to the side entrance and opened a heavy metal door leading to a set of wooden stairs that disappeared into thick gloom.

I gave him a minute, wandering around to the front of the building and looking for any sight lines into the windows, but I couldn't find a good angle. I went back to the side door and peeked inside. The stairway led into a darkness that smelled like creosote and orange-blossom tea. I knew it was a risk to go any farther, but I decided to take a chance and make a brisk foray. I took the stairs two at a time, rising quietly but quickly, and peeked around the corner of the first landing. I found an empty sitting area with a beat-up coffee table and some peeling, faux-leather couches. Down a hall, in a doorway, I could see a woman in a jumpsuit covering a chicken-wire boulder with papier-mâché. There were glossy postcards on a side table advertising art openings and personal sketching lessons. I knew this kind of place. The basic template was the same the world over. It was an art studio collective.

I hurried back outside and found a place in a doorway down the block. Now that I understood what he was doing in there, I could relax. He was inside making pictures, one of humanity's oldest distractions. I stood in the doorway at the end of a loading dock for the next three hours, enjoying the sun, watching pigeons fluxing in the sky. The flock became a fingerprint, a sail, a funnel. I watched the trucks navigating the rutted street, casting shadows that stretched around corners. I swallowed often, trying to catch the scratch in my throat, but it never quite emerged, and I called Sobie, but she didn't answer. The sky filled with enormous horse-tail clouds, followed by what looked like massive waves of rippled sand.

At last, around noon, Cave emerged and headed back the way he'd come. I didn't follow him this time. I was much more interested in his art.

I climbed the wooden stairs again, and this time the landing was populated by a handful of dissipated artist types, lounging and drinking colorful smoothies. They didn't seem to care that I was intruding. People probably came and went all the time in the building, and it was no problem because there was nothing of technical value to steal. I wandered into a long hallway, looking for the door to Cave's studio, passing a few doors with views into rooms where people painted or napped. When I came to a door with an Orozco postcard, I guessed that was the one. The door was unlocked. I slipped inside.

His studio was a humble space—a long, narrow room with a bank of frosted windows at the far end where the silhouette of a single, weedy tree moved behind the opaque glass. There was a recess to the left covered in scraps of paper, pages of magazines, sketches, and postcards. There was a bookcase filled with art tomes and collected art journals. He kept his art supplies on a high table in an orderly fashion.

His artworks covered the main walls. They were mostly faces and bodies rendered in oils, about a dozen canvases all told. The skin and hair were rough and patchy, and the space around the figures was mostly blank, just scribbles or blocks of color to suggest an environment. He was working in a pretty traditional, twentieth-century vein, it looked like, about what one would expect from someone of his age and rank. The work was interesting in part because it wasn't that interesting at all.

I photographed everything as methodically as I could with my glasses. There were other pictures, too, more cosmic and fiery, in the Orozco zone, but lacking that conviction. I tried to infer anything about his psyche from his artistic production, but the link was hard to see. He wasn't a fascist doing Greco-Roman, neoclassical figures and empty cityscapes. He wasn't a psychopath making deranged, torn-apart women. He was just a normal, late-blooming artist, drawing decent, intelligent lines, with a color sense tending to the earth tones. Pausing at each piece, I found I actually liked his work more than I might have thought. The pictures were amateurish, with bad hands, wooden postures, and harsh outlines, but I'd never been big on technical mastery.

I exited the building into the white glare of the afternoon street. As soon as I'd turned the corner and put some distance between myself and the studio, I forwarded the images to Aliyah. She called back within a minute, impressed.

"These look great, Jack," she said. "How'd you get them?"

"I went into his studio," I said.

"Actually, you know what?" she said. "I don't need to know that. I was just going to call you anyway. Do you have a minute?"

She had lots of news, it turned out. As I walked back to the hotel, she filled me in on the recent developments. The archival footage of the Trials had finally arrived, she said, and included an amazing clip of the lead prosecutor reading the accusations against Cave in absentia. You could see the chair with his name on it and everything. She'd also received an interview with a Denier hunter who called Cave the "golden fleece," and an interview with Cave's secretary from his early days at NovaChem. Things were moving fast now. We were getting close.

"I think I have a camera guy, too," she said, "if he's someone you could work with, that is."

I appreciated how she phrased it, as if my opinion really mattered. It was becoming obvious that she was the true architect of this project now, and I was only her hired agent in Mexico.

"His name is TD," she said. "He just finished shooting an interview with a warlord in Burma. Before that, he covered some mafiosos playing checkers in Singapore. This should be a pretty simple job for him. And he does his own sound, which is great for our budget."

"Super," I said. "You should hire him."

"The thing is, he's busy," she said. "He only has a small window of time. So if we want to book him, we have to make this happen on Sunday. Do you think that's possible?"

Today was Monday. That meant almost a week away. "I don't see why not," I said.

"Good," she said. "Then he'll fly down on Saturday night and you guys can meet and talk this through. And in the morning you'll make your move and do the Donaldson. We're almost there, Jack. If you can just hold on a little longer we'll be on the other side."

I hung up and kept walking, measuring the new timeline in my mind. Monday. Saturday arrival; Sunday, the Donaldson. The eclipse was Friday. A flight took five or six hours, depending on layover. A drive to the ocean took about three hours. Within half a block I was calling Sobie. If she could get the days off, I told her, I'd buy her a ticket.

10

Cave visited the museum most weekdays, usually in the late morning or early afternoon. He went to his studio most weekdays, too, usually in the early morning, and occasionally taught a class at the elementary school in the late afternoon. He went to an old-school gym three days a week, late in the day, where he trained like a boxer, jumping rope and punching the heavy bag. Fish night on Wednesday with Maggie was an immutable fact.

Unfortunately, that left weekends fairly open-ended. If Sunday was our day of confrontation and we wanted control over the time and place, I was going to have to arrange some kind of meeting in advance.

The museum seemed like the obvious location for the Donaldson. It was grandly picturesque, quiet, and contained the whole history of our encounter, going all the way back to the first sighting by Jeff Catalog. Abstractly, the museum was also the repository

of cultural memory. It spoke of stewardship, institutional conti-
nuity, power, justice. This particular museum even had the bones
of extinct animals in the collection. It just worked on many levels.
If we confronted Cave there, we could interrogate him in the
hushed, well-lit sanctum of the café. And if he refused to talk, we
could follow him all the way home, peppering him with further
questions, eliciting as many denials as he was willing to give.

The trick was getting him to appear at the museum at the
right time. For that, I needed an excuse. I needed to tempt him
out, to offer an invitation that appealed to his interests and also
his ego. His interests were art, sports, and history, as far as I could
tell. He liked staying inside the walking radius of his general
neighborhood. What could it be?

Bullfights happened on Sundays. And the Plaza de Toros
was only about a half-hour walk from the museum. I looked at
the week's listings and found a perfect event, ready-made. On
Sunday morning, a once-famous matador would be returning
to the ring. He'd been widely revered in his prime, but his last
appearance had ended in a shameful debacle. His assistants had
pre-bled the bull much more than usual, which had been bad
enough, but the matador had still failed to make the kill on
the first two passes. On his third attempt, he'd sunk his sword
but missed the sweet spot between the shoulder blades, merely
wounding the animal. His aides had been forced to run into
the ring and deliver a killing blow to the head. The crowd had
booed for twenty minutes straight.

Sunday would be his chance for redemption. The local bull-fighting threads were ablaze with excitement and speculation. The fight started at 11:00 a.m., which meant I could ask Cave to meet me at the museum at 10:00 a.m. and guide me through the whole cultural experience. We'd never make it to the arena, sadly, but that was all right. I could read all about the fight in Monday's paper.

*　　*　　*

Cave's face lit up as soon as he saw me in the café. I was sitting at my regular seat, drinking my regular order, sending off signals of easy familiarity and welcome. Once he had his coffee in hand, he came directly over to wish me a happy new year.

"How was Cabo?" I said, making room at the table.

"Absurd," he said, taking off his coat. "Maggie is right. It's a terrible place. We'll never go again."

"That's too bad," I said. "I hope the weather was nice at least."

"It was fine," he said. "We saw a pod of gray whales on our last day. That was the highlight, I'd say. That was quite incredible, in fact."

He sat down and held forth about the migration patterns of whales. They birthed their calves in Baja and migrated to Alaska every year, he said, which constituted one of the longest maritime migrations in the world. They traveled over twelve thousand miles in all, and the trip kept getting longer as the ice caps receded. On the way north, the new mothers hugged the shoreline with their new calves in tow, fending off orcas and stray fishing nets, while the bulls made the trip later, not helping in the least.

As he talked, I kept on the lookout for any opportunities to bring up the bullfight. I didn't want to force the subject, but I didn't want to wait too long, either. If the invitation failed, I'd have to think of another strategy. At the very least, I wanted to come away with his coordinates on Sunday. So at the first lull in conversation, apropos of nothing, I went ahead and mentioned the bullfight and my interest in his company.

"Bullfight, eh," he said. "Not too many gringos going to bull-fights these days. What makes you want to witness that form of barbarity?"

"I want to see one while I still have the chance," I said. "They won't be around much longer, from what I understand."

"Oh, they'll be around," he said. "Don't worry about that. People complain about them, but the bullfight is one of human-ity's most ancient rituals. At the very beginning of civilization, men were encircling a plot of dirt and watching other men kill bulls. I imagine they'll be doing it at the very end, too."

"That's a depressing thought," I said.

"Is it?" he said. "No one even protests them down here anymore. People realized they'd just go underground. They'd become like cockfights. Even worse. At least this way there's some regulation. The meat still goes to the poor."

"Well, I'm planning to go this Sunday," I said. "If you're interested, I'd love a good guide."

Cave seemed to mull the invitation. He stared off into the room for a moment, retrieving a memory or imagining some future, I couldn't tell which. When he came back to me, he had his answer:

"Of course," he said. "I'd love to go. I haven't seen a bullfight in quite some time."

So it was agreed. The backstory about the matador's redemption hadn't even been necessary. We would meet on Sunday and walk to the arena from the café. After that, we enjoyed another hour of rambling, amiable conversation, nursing our coffees, eating our pastries. For the first time, Cave showed some interest in my own life history. He asked me questions about my youth in Ohio, and I told him about my old neighbors, and the trees that now covered my childhood territory. For twenty years, I said, the government had been planting trees in the region by the thousands—tough, weed-like varieties, and hardwoods, species intended to endure whatever climate came next. At this point, every empty lot and side street had been seeded, and the early saplings had matured into stately trunks. When I went home now, I didn't recognize a thing. My childhood had been swallowed by a forest.

He asked me about Sobie, too, and I gave him the whole story of our meeting in the optometry department. I told him about our past together and even mentioned her voice, her eyes.

I rarely talked openly about personal matters like that, but on this day, I did. I was under the assumption that it was best to tell as much truth as possible when lying. Bury the lies in piles of truth, I thought. In the end, I even told him about our plan to see the Totality. Anything to keep Cave from suspecting what was really happening.

"Wonderful," he said, pleased by the news of my romantic fortune. "Meeting for the second time is always the best. That's when you know something is meant to be. Where are you going for the eclipse, exactly?"

"To the beach," I said. "A town called San Blas. Not too far."

"Wonderful place," he said. "Terrible mosquitos, but beautiful jungle there. There's an old hotel on the coastline. They rebuilt it around the turn of the century. It's worth a look."

"I'll put that on our list," I said.

Soon, our coffee was finished, and our plates were empty. A square of sun had edged onto our table, brightening the single zinnia in a glass. I started putting away my phone and book— *Tom Sawyer*—and we began our parting formalities. I told Cave to please say hello to Maggie for me. He told me she sent her best. He asked me what the rest of my day held. I told him I still had to rent a car, among other travel duties.

"You don't have a car yet?" he said.

"Not yet," I said.

"There are no cars to rent in Jalisco," he said.

"You don't think so?" I said.

He shook his head definitively. "There are two million people coming to Mexico for the Totality," he said. "You can't get a car now."

"Oh," I said, and immediately started babbling about other options. We could take a bus, I said, or a taxi, or some kind of ride-share deal, but even as I listed off the ideas, I could see that none of them were remotely plausible. I hadn't thought about the car. And because Guadalajara wasn't in the actual zone of Totality, if we didn't get out of the city, we'd miss the whole thing.

"Why don't you just use my car?" Cave said.

"Oh, I couldn't do that," I said.

"I have a car that I almost never use," he said. "It could stand a little workout. You'd be doing me a favor."

"Oh. I don't know," I said.

"Absolutely," he said. "Come on. We can get it right now. I'm not that far from here."

I paused, unsure what to do. Refusing such a flagrant act of generosity would seem insane, I realized. It would possibly even come as an affront. The offer he was making was about more than just the car, I could see. He was offering me his friendship, extending a credit that we could begin trading back and forth, possibly in perpetuity. To refuse the car would in a sense be to refuse him. If I wanted to keep him on the line, I saw, I had to accept.

"I don't know what to say," I said. "Thank you."

*   *   *

We walked to Cave's house to get the car. On the way I acted as if the streets we traveled were all new to me and I'd never seen any of the various landmarks he pointed out before. The bar where the local businessmen gathered, the park where the fountain sprayed, the playground with the enormous, treacherous-looking climbing structure, all of it I pretended had never passed before my eyes.

We turned onto his block and proceeded to his address, the now-familiar two-story box with the red ceramic tile roof. Earlier in the week, I'd traced the building's line of ownership, which I'd discovered involved various shell companies and blind trusts and predictably dropped into an abyss on the edge of the Cayman Islands. It was something I'd definitely be asking him about on Sunday.

"Beautiful place," I said. "You've been here a long time?"

"Pretty long," he said. "It's humble, but it's home."

Cave unlocked the gate with a wireless fob in his pocket. There was a high buzzing whine and a heavy metallic click. We pushed through the iron gate and walked into a yard of raked dirt surrounding a few picturesque rocks. Fallen seedpods and stray leaves littered the Zen-like furrows, and a jasmine tree cast a maze of shadows. We climbed the steps, and Cave opened the front door into the cool maw of the interior.

I entered behind him, taking in the scene. The decor in the entryway and what I could see of the living room was tasteful, well-organized, and warmly brown. The walls were painted a cool taupe. The tiles visible in the kitchen were dark chocolate. The furniture was antique mid-century, cherry and teak, and the artwork was modern, with a handmade, Mesoamerican flavor. Cave was a man alone who managed to exert fine taste in his domain. He continued to impress.

"The car needs to charge," he said. "It doesn't take very long. Come on. This way."

I followed him to a side door and into a narrow carport where his car was parked. The car was a thing of incredible beauty—a giant, emerald green stone freshly pulled from a mountain stream. The snout was mildly pointed, sharklike, and the back was mildly flared, so the whole object had the satisfying curves of a squared-off egg. Up in the US, people were into these retro, Deco lines lately, I'd noticed, but down in Mexico they were still rare. The charging stations were only starting to stitch into a usable network.

"The batteries they have now are incredible," Cave said, as if answering my thoughts, plugging the car in to feed from solar panels on the roof. "This guy can go over two thousand miles on a single charge. They don't have a lot of stations down here, but with this ultracapacitor, you don't need to worry. You can get to the beach and back three times if you needed to, and even if you ran out of juice you'd be okay. I haven't tried it yet, but they say the battery can be charged from space. Can you believe that?"

He leaned in the door and checked the battery's gauge on the control panel. "It still needs a few minutes," he said. "Coffee?"

We went back into the muffled tranquility of his cool, beige house. He made us coffee, and we sat down in the dining room, at a teak table beside a sliding glass door covered in a sheer curtain with the lightest saffron tint. On the table was a vase with yellow tropical lilies. It was an arrangement that invited contemplation.

Mostly, we talked about the car. He clearly enjoyed talking about the advanced engineering it contained. The body's shell was made out of a carbon fiber forged from a polymer strong enough to withstand a direct hit from an eighteen-wheeler. The interior was upholstered in synthetic leather almost indistinguishable from real cowhide, and the onboard computer had the navigation capacity of a NASA satellite. It could give you CPR if you needed it. Not that he used any of that somatic tech. He was a privacy freak, he said, and didn't like sharing any genetic data with the mother ship if he could possibly avoid it. As such, he'd disabled as much of the feedback loop as possible, so we'd be on our own in that regard, but he could switch on the guest function to give me access to most of the navigation devices. He passed me the key control, a polymer disk the size of a silver dollar. He said I wouldn't need anything else.

"They said we couldn't break the fossil fuel habit," he said, sipping his coffee, marveling again at the car's design. "But they were wrong. The car is a wonder. It's remarkable how humanity can adapt. Thank God for the Upheavals, I say."

I wasn't sure how to respond to that. From most people I knew, Cave's sentiment would have been fairly normal. Most of them loved nothing more than expressing their nostalgia for the days of transformation, the explosion of solidarity that had been so undeniable, righteous, and interesting. It had been the crux of our adult lives, most all agreed. Solidarity with air! Solidarity with earth! We still signed off with those words, the level of irony attached depending.

Next usually came the reflexive cynicism and consternation about all the failed promises. The sellouts, the backstabbers, the compromisers all too happy to leave the status quo intact. It was a subject to avoid unless you were among close friends, I'd found. The schismatics were still tricky to navigate. But coming from Cave, Denier in hiding, the words held a different weight altogether. They seemed like a test.

"Some might say they went a little far," I said. I didn't want to push him too hard, but I was curious what else he might divulge. I was even seeing a small opening toward the jackpot of tearful, guilty confession. It would alter our Donaldson plans, but it would be worth it. My glasses, as always, were recording the scene.

"I don't think so," he said. "Not far enough. In my opinion."

"Hanging Jared Curtis?" I said. "Life imprisonment for Bowen? Those were some very severe sentences for guys who didn't actually kill anyone. They were just executives. Bureau-crats."

"So was Göring," he said. "So was Himmler. The Toronto gang killed whole phylums. Someone had to be held account-able for all that carnage. That's how justice works. We choose someone and make an example so we know the limits. Those people stood for many. Someone had to be the representative."

He smiled, as if nothing could be more uncontroversial. We were stepping into an odd, irradiated landscape now. Strange shadows were falling. It was like we'd swapped masks and I was taking his role, he was taking mine. But did he know we'd swapped masks? I didn't know if he knew or not. This was either an act of supreme arrogance on his part or supreme vulnerability, I couldn't tell.

"They were only doing what we asked them to do," I said. "They were feeding us what we wanted. We all burned the gas. We all ate the meat. But they paid a price for it. Maybe we should all pay a little more."

He nodded, but not in agreement. "I hear what you're say-ing," he said. "I've had those arguments with myself. You don't blame the hand for a murder. You blame the whole human being. The mind and body conspire. The system as a whole is at fault. But as a species, we had to make a statement. We had to draw a line."

Cave went on, in a more ruminative tone. "I didn't under-stand it clearly myself at the time," he said. "I was as bad as any of them. I thought we had to feed the fire or the whole machine would blow up, the furnace would go cold. It was the way I was raised. I assumed we had no other way."

"But you changed your mind?" I said.

"I didn't understand how change occurred back then," he said. "I look back and it's incredible to think how we used to function. We once blocked rivers and burned gas and coal to run our grids. One giant dam piping the energy everywhere? One giant nuke plant? That seems so crude now, so stupid, when you can just harvest energy anywhere in little packets. A cell here, a cell there. Who knew we had to go back to the days of the textile mill with the spinning water wheel? Little turbines everywhere. Why didn't that make sense to me in 2025?"

"It didn't make sense to a lot of people," I said. "You can't blame people for their misperceptions. It was widespread."

"No, I think you can," he said. "That's the lesson of Toronto, isn't it? Willful ignorance is no defense. Denial is an act of will. The Toronto gang was engaged in a systematic assault on life on earth. They were profiteering from it, sowing disinformation. It was a death cult. You could say a lot of other people deserved to be on trial, sure. It could have been billions of people on trial. But everyone on that docket definitely deserved what they got."

"Not everyone got what they deserved," I said. We were standing on the cusp between deception and reality itself now. Would he reveal himself? Would he recognize my intentions? The air itself seemed to throb, on the verge of rending.

"I suppose," he said.

"What about the ones who got away?" I said, taking us another step.

"What about them?" he said. "The people on trial represented organizations. The names were arbitrary."

"But why stop there?" I said. "Why not indict the whole boards? The stockholders?"

"That's childish," he said. "You can't indict everyone. And anyway, they'll all be judged someday. Even the consumers."

"You think so?" I said.

"No," he said, and laughed. "A lot passes beneath notice. Some people escape judgment altogether. People would like to think there's some kind of justice in the universe, a grand arc toward equality or fairness or something, but what in the world would suggest that's true? Justice. I don't think so."

"So did Toronto really change anything, then?" I said. "Or not?" This was a genuine question I asked myself daily. Had anything been won? Had society progressed? Or had the chairs simply been shuffled? I looked around most days and it seemed like nothing had changed. I'd read that very morning about a junta in Africa secretly fracking its mountain ranges. The global coalition's satellite had discovered the sites, and there was nothing anyone could do.

"Something changed," he said. "Most definitely, something changed. We changed, as a society. As a species, we evolved."

"I wonder sometimes," I said.

"We did," he said, without any inkling of doubt in his voice. "Individually, we became smaller. We became more like ants. And collectively, we became stronger, more conscious. We became stronger, and we became less free."

*   *   *

The car finished charging. Cave guided me out of his narrow alleyway and sent me off with good cheer, tapping the hood, telling me to enjoy the drive, take my time. Pulling away, watching him in the rearview, I couldn't help but feel like a teenager taking off in Dad's car.

Sobie's plane didn't arrive until the morning, so I had time for a little spin around the city to get used to the car's torque. The engine had good pickup, a charging, silent thrust at the slightest touch, and the tires cornered sweetly. The dashboard was pleasingly simple, only a single, modest screen on the window, and the leather smell from the padded seats was mildly intoxicating. I enjoyed the looks I got from the men and children on the sidewalk, flying around in my green seed.

Driving through the streets, I wondered if Cave had been trying to tell me something in there. Had that been his confession? If so, it was an elegantly inexplicit one at best. He hadn't really confessed to anything, except crimes of thought. I'd have to dig pretty deeply into his words to find anything that might be considered remorse.

Or possibly it was all just a feint. He might have been speaking directly to the camera. Maybe he already knew exactly who I was. He was already talking to the judge, saying: I'm reformed. I've changed. He was a few steps ahead yet again. Or maybe he really meant what he'd said. He'd come to see the world in a different light. He knew he was lucky that he'd slipped the noose. And his good fortune had changed his heart.

I was pretty sure he had no idea what was happening. He had no idea that in a matter of days he'd be revealed to the world and hauled away and jailed by the global legal bureaucracy. He didn't know he'd very likely die in prison, that his life would be destroyed, wholly this time.

I imagined Cave in jail, eating cubes of plankton protein in his gray prison uniform. I imagined Maggie devastated in her beautiful apartment. I imagined his son, tragically triumphant, wherever he was. I imagined his ex-wife, the elementary school students, his studio mates, all abandoned. What would be gained by his punishment? I asked myself. I searched for anger and indignation in myself and didn't find much.

I drove up to a hilltop overlooking the city and stopped at a park where clumps of eucalyptus and cactus grew. The trees were stunted, and a wide view of the city's lights shimmered in the dusk. The sky was blood brown, streaked with orange and pink. A palm frond shifted in the breeze. I left the car on the shoulder and walked to a stone wall a few hundred yards away to sit down, unsure how far the car's halo of surveillance extended. I didn't trust Cave wasn't watching me.

I gazed at the city in the gathering darkness below. My body wasn't in any kind of pain. My brain was working fine. Even my rash was quiet. The sky dimmed further, and a few pinpoints appeared in the haze, but only the strongest ones, the planets.

11

Before Sobie arrived the next morning, I went to an outdoor store and got us two cheap sleeping bags, a flashlight, and snorkeling masks. After that, I went to the grocery store and bought a twenty-four pack of bottled water and a few bags of regular potato chips. I also bought coffee filters, a solar water-heating device, a frying pan, and two mugs. I felt strange, buying all the materials I'd only use one time, but I figured I could allow myself the extravagance. We were going to witness a once-in-a-lifetime astronomical event. And relative to most people, my footprint was still very light.

I piled the gear into the green seed's tiny trunk and went back to the hotel and packed my own bag. By then it was midmorning, and I went into the kitchenette to fix my regular egg and toast. I pulled a slice of bread from the refrigerator and put it in the toaster, turned on the stovetop, and wiped a pat of butter in the skillet. I went to grab the eggs out of the refrigerator, but this time, for some reason, the eggs weren't there.

That's strange, I thought. I could've sworn I'd just bought some eggs. I distinctly remembered refusing the fake-biodegradable bag at the store and carrying the carton in my hand on the way home. Or so I thought I remembered.

I looked in the refrigerator again, but there was only half a loaf of bread, a container of yogurt, and a bottle of hot sauce. I turned around and looked on the counter and the tabletop. The eggs weren't there, either. The butter was sizzling, and I turned off the stove, puzzled.

The toast popped. I buttered the toast. I ate the toast, still scanning for my eggs. Maybe I hadn't bought the eggs after all. Maybe I was remembering a different trip to the store. The memory was soft and scruffy around the edges. I remembered walking in and out of shadows with the eggs. I remembered traffic sounds. I was on the verge of giving up and having another piece of toast when I spotted the eggs on top of the refrigerator. I must have put them there on one of my rounds, but I had no memory of doing so.

Light seemed to collect on the carton of eggs. Every detail became articulated, all the divots and scratches in the grain of the reused, molded paper pulp. I sat down on the edge of my bed and looked at the egg carton from across the room.

I didn't usually lose things, or even misplace things. I definitely didn't forget things in the middle of using them. I wasn't exactly tidy, but underneath my messes there was usually a fundamental order. I kept my shoes on a stand next to the door and placed my wallet and keys in the same small bowl on the bookshelf every night. I stored my tools in a special box inside a special drawer. I labeled my cooking spices. My control over inanimate objects was a source of daily pleasure, to the point where I'd re-created my little piles down in Mexico. Every evening, my objects went into their places; every morning, they were collected.

If the eggs had been the only memory lapse lately, I wouldn't have worried about it. But I knew it was only the most recent in a growing string. A few days earlier, I'd walked onto the street holding my toothbrush in my hand. A day before that, I'd forgotten my bank password of thirty years. The eggs were part of an emerging pattern.

I sat on my bed, staring at the eggs. I couldn't help imagining the prions inside my eyes, folding away. They were burrowing down in my body by now, devouring the fibers and tendons, eating into my very bones. When I closed my eyes, I saw them dancing in the blackness, a million bent, glowing sticks. They flashed and shivered, almost taunting me.

I breathed evenly. In my mind, I tried to reach out and isolate one of the prions. If I could unbend one, I thought, I might heal myself. If I could just straighten the prions in my mind, hammer them back into shape, the problem would be solved. It became a kind of game, reaching into the tangle of imaginary sticks and unbending them one by one. Eventually I had a nice pile of straight lines in my head. Soon I rose and made myself an egg. What else could I do?

*   *   *

The road to the airport was a mess of cars, scooters, and brightly painted buses. The grandfathered diesel hogs poured clouds of exhaust. The tinny motorcycles whizzed in and out of every gap. Cars swerved back and forth between barely marked lanes. I almost smashed into a pickup truck hauling a new washing machine and almost sideswiped a shuttle bus with a broken back window, but somehow every accident was narrowly averted. It was like the traffic had its own collective mind, its own binding intuition.

I motored onward to Terminal 3 and spotted Sobie in the crowd on the arrivals deck. She was about fifty yards down the breezeway, scanning the cars, looking a little confused, but cool enough not to show it. Eclipse tourists of many origins passed behind her, dragging their luggage, hailing their cabs, and as I got closer, I could see she looked a little tired. Her eyes were bagged, and her coat was crooked around her neck. In a way, it only added to her allure. She'd been through something. She had something to tell me.

I pulled up and wrestled her bags into the back seat, and we exchanged a quick, chaste peck. It wasn't exactly the reunion

I'd imagined, but it was the best we could do. People were honking.

It was only after we'd merged onto the highway and tucked in behind a lumbering cement truck that we were finally able to settle down and acknowledge each other as people.

"You're here," I said.

"I made it," she said.

"Flight was okay?" I said.

"It was all right," she said.

"But not that great?" I said.

"Honestly, it was kind of terrible," she said.

She told me about the trip. The guy next to her on the plane had taken up way too much space, she said. He was gigantic, even by American standards. His legs didn't fit in the foot area, and his arms covered the whole armrest. Also, he smelled bad. Every time he moved she'd gotten this whiff, like onions and hamsters. She'd had to turn her face away and breathe into her shoulder the whole time, which was why she hadn't been able to get any sleep and her neck hurt.

"Someone needs to tell that guy he has a problem," she said. "Not me. It isn't my job. But someone who cares about him. They really should tell him somehow. It's a hard one, I know, telling someone that. But they should."

She was trying to maintain good spirits, but I could tell she was anxious about being so far from home. I didn't blame her.

She'd embarked on a sudden, strange voyage, and whatever last-minute organizing she'd had to do for the babysitter, the dog walker, the client list, was still turning in her head. It was going to take a while to put the day's beginning behind her.

Sobie turned away and stared at the passing city. Signs for hotels, storage space, and grocery stores approached and receded, and off in the distance, the grimy silhouettes of Guadalajara's skyscrapers hovered, obscured by gray smog.

"Have you ever been to Mexico before?" I said.

"No," she said. "Costa Rica once. And Argentina. I knew people with a goat farm in Argentina. I worked there for a few months. None of that's the same thing, though, I know."

"Guadalajara is a really beautiful city," I said. "Not this part. But other parts."

"I can imagine."

She returned to watching. Over the phone, the conversation between us always flowed easily, but sitting together in a car, physically close, the distance seemed to widen. There was too much to process in person. Her fingernails and the curve of her neck, for instance. I told myself it was all normal enough. It was just going to take a minute to get back in sync, to let our bodies remember each other in space.

The onboard navigator guided us through the highway interchanges. We nearly missed a few off-ramps but finally hit a straight, westward course. We didn't bother talking anymore—we understood silence was easier—and the city continued

DENIAL

sprawling. We passed miles of low, jerry-rigged neighborhoods and dusty barrios until the denser construction broke up into ellipses of outlying developments. We crossed a valley of modular slums, immense factory towns built around distant juice factories and slaughterhouses. After that, finally, the landscape started to appear in larger eyefuls, in the form of red earth, hardy cactus, windswept grass.

"Pretty," she said.

We began to climb. The earth lifted us over the buildings and into the air, and after cresting a massive berm we shed the city altogether. We were moving onto the high plains now, out into the desert and the brown sky. The landscape was a wasteland of brown flats behind a never-ending fence. The sun was a hot smudge in the smoky particulate, and the surrounding air was mostly yellow. On the horizon, a haze of smoke and dust floated low to the ground.

"I hope we can even see the eclipse," she said. "Is it going to be like this the whole time?"

"This is worse than usual," I said. "There are wildfires to the east right now. They say the wind is going to shift in the next couple days. We should be fine."

"I hope they're right," she said. "I could see a bunch of smoke at home."

We passed a bloated dead horse, its legs pointing at the sky, then another. In a half hour we passed five horse corpses. They looked like they might explode at the slightest touch.

"God," she said. "Why do they leave them out like that?"

"They don't have an animal control department down here," I said. "There's no one to pick them up."

"They should get someone," she said.

"They have a different attitude about it, I guess," I said. "They're more comfortable seeing that kind of thing."

"I don't want to see it," she said. "Why would I? No thank you. Awful. I mean, that's a horse."

An hour into the drive, Sobie fell asleep. She snored softly as we glided over the smoky plain, whipping by small groups of Indians gathering twigs alongside the road. There were no structures in sight, or even land formations. I didn't see any vehicles, or pack animals, either. They pulled simple wagons piled with kindling, and nothing else.

We left them behind, but they stayed in my mind. I imagined the men and women going home at the end of the day to a village of thatched huts. Or maybe adobe apartments built into an arroyo wall. I imagined young boys pulling clean water from a stream in ceramic pots, women mashing maize in stone bowls. I imagined little girls braiding cotton thread into colorful tapestries. I had no idea how these people really lived, so my mind filled with stock fantasies I'd picked up from documentaries and magazines.

I was still deep in my daydream when the tire blew. I didn't even notice it at first. There was no explosion or sudden twist of the wheel. At some point I started hearing that telltale *thwup*

thwup sound and feeling the mild tug, the bumping turbulence. It might've been going on for a while for all I knew.

I pulled over onto the shoulder, and as the car slowed Sobie awakened. She understood without asking that some mechanical problem had occurred. We both got out of the car, and dust swam onto the seats. The air was heavy with the smell of burning grass and wildflowers and sage. We walked around the car and discovered the front passenger-side tire was pancaked.

"Great," I said.

"That's no good," she said.

"All the tech in the world," I said, "and a simple tire fucks you."

"Can you fix it?" she said.

"There's no spare," I said. "The car is too small to carry one. And Cave shut off all the sensors."

"So what do people do?" she said.

"In the US, they'd call the manufacturer and a drone would bring one. Or your insurance would have some roadside assistance plan. But down here, I don't know."

"So what do we do?" she said.

I got down on my knees and made an effort to inspect the damage, but I could barely do that much. The design of the car's exterior shell made it almost impossible to access the wheel wells. The tires were covered in a metal sheath that didn't seem to have a seam.

"I can't even get to the tire," I said.

"Hmm," she said.

"There were some buildings a mile or so back," I said, standing and brushing off the dust. "We can drive on it that far, at least."

So we turned around and drove down the road to investigate. We went slowly, not wanting to damage the car any more than we already had, and as we approached, we saw that thankfully one of the buildings in the cluster was a garage. Unfortunately, it was closed. Everything among this collection of buildings was closed. It was only two o'clock and the whole town was desolate.

We parked in the dirt lot in front of the garage.

"You think anyone is here?" she said.

We got out and walked around the lot, peering into the gaps in the fence. Our footsteps were enormous, crushing the silence. The fence was part wood, part chain link, the top frosted with barbed wire. There were a lot of ruined cars in there, dented and disassembled and parked without any order. There were also chickens and one of those hairless Mexican dogs they said dated to the Aztecs. The cars were old El Caminos, old Foresters, old Priuses, old Vibes, a junkyard of internal combustion machines at least three generations deep. Someone was under the impression the carcasses of these vehicles might still be worth something.

Down the street a door opened and a woman tossed a bucket of water on the dust. The door led into a restaurant that hadn't looked open before, but now it was, so we walked over and checked out the scene. It was a little diner—a bare room with a handful of wooden tables covered in plastic tablecloths, with hard metal chairs and saltshakers half-filled with rice to suck out the humidity. An older woman in an apron with roosters on it was energetically chopping serrano peppers. She seemed to be the owner, waitress, and cook.

"Abierto?" I said.

"Sí, sí," she said, and waved us in. We took a table on the wall and looked over the menu. It was too early for dinner, and too late for lunch, but we decided to order the comida cor-rida—chicken enchiladas. The owner took our orders, and I tried prying some information from her about the garage down the street. Unfortunately, for all my time in Mexico, my Spanish was still crude.

"Esta?" I pointed in the direction of the garage. "Es para camions?" I had almost no idea what I was saying, or even what I was trying to ask. I was just trying to throw some words out there and give her the chance to tell me what she knew.

"Sí."

"Y . . . quando abierto?"

A flurry of language came back, with hand gestures and elab-orate, kindly intonations. Sobie and I both nodded, pretending we understood much more than we did. The woman finished her statement and went back to the kitchen and didn't come back for a long time. Sobie and I agreed it seemed like she'd been saying the garage would open tomorrow.

" 'Mañana,' she said," Sobie said. "I think she said the owner is in the city. 'Ciudad.' I heard that word."

"Or he committed suicide," I said. " 'Ciudad.' 'Suicide.' "

"She didn't seem very sad about it if he committed suicide," she said.

"That's true," I said.

"Enemies."

Eventually, the woman came back bearing the food, but it turned out not to be chicken enchiladas. Instead, she placed two large plates of beefsteak on our table. The menu was old, she communicated. That was last week's menu. The menu didn't mean anything anyway.

I peered at two long, brown strips of meat swimming in greasy, watery fluid. The meat was covered in soft peppers, buttressed by a pile of orange rice and a puddle of refried beans, American-style. I hadn't eaten meat like this since I was a child.

"This isn't what we wanted," Sobie said, as the woman disappeared.

"I know," I said.

"I can't eat this," she said.

"Yeah," I said.

"But it seems kind of rude not to," she said.

"It's fine," I said. "You don't have to eat it."

"Are you going to eat it?"

I looked at the strips of meat, grained with muscle. The outermost layer was browned, but just underneath the meat looked gray. "It's what people eat here," I said. "They've eaten it for a long time."

"I know," she said. "But people have raped and enslaved each other for a long time, too. That's not a good argument."

"I feel like I should try it," I said. "To be polite. We're in a different country. You want to be a good guest."

"I don't think I can, though," she said.

"I don't want it to go to waste," I said.

She sighed. "My parents loved hamburgers."

"So did mine."

We both looked at our enormous plates.

"Well," I said. "Here I go."

"Okay, I'll try it, too."

We cut pieces of the beefsteak and put them in our mouths. I felt like a cannibal, it'd been so long. I chewed the meat, tasting grass, dirt, and distinct hoof. Two bites in and I saw the cow's face in my mind, as clear as Sobie's across the table. I saw its wet nose speckled with mud and its crusted eyelashes. I could tell Sobie was struggling, too.

"I can't do this," she said.

"No. Me neither."

We concentrated on the beans and rice instead. We had a basket of warm tortillas on the table and a bowl of pickled carrots and peppers. That was enough. When the owner passed by, we pretended everything was fine and changed the topic by asking her if there was a hotel nearby. I closed my eyes and rested my cheek on my hands to make the sleeping gesture. The woman shook her head. No, no, she said. This area, she seemed to say, was not a place for that.

We ordered soft drinks to keep paying rent on the chairs and drifted into the deep dead zone of late afternoon. A man shuffled into the room at some point, her husband, possibly. She gave him some blunt orders, and he exited. A teenage girl and a little girl appeared and departed. Two flies killed time with us, buzzing along their idiot pathways.

"Imagine living here," I said.

"I can't," Sobie said.

"To be alone all the time," I said. "It might be all right."

"I'm never alone," she said. "That isn't really possible for me."

"You mean you can't imagine being alone?" I said.

"No, I mean I'm never alone," she said. "Even here, I'd never be alone. I'm a mom."

The owner came back to the table and said something to us that we didn't understand. She said it a second time and we still didn't catch her meaning, so she took Sobie by the hand and pulled her onto her feet.

"Vamos," she said, which we understood.

She walked us deeper into the restaurant, past the register and into the kitchen, where there was a double grill and many metal containers stacked on the far wall. A few pots simmered on the burners, one half-filled with beans, another with menudo.

On the floor was a rubber mat that seemed coated in lard. It was better not to look down there.

We exited the kitchen and walked down a narrow hallway to a room in the back of the building. The doorway was a yellow sheet. In the room was a naked double bed.

The owner pointed to the bed and shrugged. It seemed like she was making an offer. We could sleep there if we wanted.

"Quanto?" I said. "Para una noche."

She shrugged. Five hundred pesos? It was about $10.

The room seemed fairly clean, and it would definitely beat sleeping in the car. Sobie and I exchanged a game look and agreed to stay the night. We tried to express to the woman how grateful we were for her generosity, but she seemed to think it was nothing. It was just what a person should do.

*   *   *

We still had some hours to go before sleeping, so we ambled around the town, such as it was, checking the vistas. To the south, nothing; to the west, nothing. Same in every direction. The expanse of dust and dead grass seemed endless. Up above, the sky was finally clearing, and the pale blue vaulting beyond the smoke was coming through. Soon the sun was streaming sideways through the town, casting long, knifing shadows across the blanched earth. It was like some whistle had sounded, and a few people materialized, along with a few dogs and a few chickens. At last, the creatures who lived here were coming out. They stayed in their holes all day and emerged only for that last, sad, lonely moment.

"I should call Eileen," Sobie said as the night poured in, and wandered away with her phone. Within a few steps she was deep in conversation and I was alone. I couldn't figure what to do without her. I had nothing to look at, nothing to touch. I needed something to distract me, so I started throwing rocks. I made a target out of a pile of rocks and collected a pile of rock ammunition. I paced off twenty feet or so and took aim, threw, heard the rock strike rock. I threw again, enjoying the tiny clatter.

Off in the distance, I could hear Sobie talking to her daughter. The conversation came in ragged bits, torn apart by the wind. The conversation went on for a few minutes, sprinkled with occasional laughter, while I tossed the rocks. I watched a chicken banging its head against the dirt.

When Sobie came back, she didn't seem that pleased. The laughter she'd projected into the phone was no longer happening. We stood there in silence. A few stars were visible. She had to be wondering what she was doing out here, so far from where she'd begun her day. Hours ago she'd been in her own living room, surrounded by her own things. Now she was standing where?

"Maybe I'll get to meet Eileen someday," I said. "I hope so."

"That would be nice," she said. But there was nothing resembling any kind of promise in her voice.

The air was getting colder, and we went back to the restaurant and ate again. This time we only ordered tortillas and beans and rice, which we spiced up with more pickled carrots and jalapeños. The food was simple but decent, and overall the night-time mood of the diner was a little brighter than the afternoon. Mariachi music played on the jukebox, and incredibly, another white couple wandered in from somewhere in the desert. They appeared to be Mennonites from one of the communities in the area. They'd been there for generations, I'd heard. The husband wore a beard and a dirty cowboy hat. The wife wore a bonnet and a floor-length skirt. They sat down at a table across the room. They wanted nothing to do with us.

*   *   *

We went to bed early. The room smelled like motor oil, and the bed was cold, and the sheets were greasy. We spotted a few bugs on the walls, strange creatures with elaborate horns and scimitar legs, which we hoped were friendly. We huddled close and tried to keep warm. There was nothing remotely sexual going on this evening, not in the cold back room of this campesino woman's diner on the plain.

We lay there as the building settled in the night. Wind oozed into the cracks in the high window. The sound of trucks bellowed on the highway, shaking the room every few minutes. The headlights ripped along the uppermost edge of the curtain, orange comets streaming just out of view. We could hear the jangling chains, the rubberized friction of all that weight careening down the road and roaring onward into the distance.

We didn't talk, and in between the passing vehicles the silence condensed into an almost physical substance. The air became crystalline, vibrating against our ears. We could hear bugs crawling on the floor. We could hear the movement of the clouds. And then, ineluctably, the sound began again, far away, a low premonition at first, almost beyond audibility, rising to a whine, and gradually a roar, until the hurtling mass of the object blasted by, receding into another all-encompassing silence.

We shouldn't have come, I thought. We were here together, lying in the same bed, but we were drifting ever further apart. We were floating further and further into our own thoughts, our own concerns. My rash was itching almost down to my knee, and the warm tickle in my throat was worse than before. I didn't want to say anything because it wasn't fair to Sobie. I didn't want to drag her into that spiral with me. She hadn't signed up for that.

I could hear her breathing next to me, but I didn't think she was asleep. She was just lying still, basting in her own thoughts, peering into her own darkness. I could feel her weight on the mattress as she shifted and rolled over onto her back. She let out a sigh. I thought she'd turn over again, away from me, but she stayed where she was. A moment later her hand found mine and our fingers clasped. A few minutes later she was asleep.

12

It was midmorning by the time the mechanic showed up. He was a middle-aged man with a paunchy swagger, big, flashing teeth, and a little English. Although fixing a tire seemed far below his interest level, the car itself was appealing. It was a rare object of advanced tech in this empty zone.

He called over a younger friend, and together they admired the car's lines. They especially appreciated the polymer coating on the exterior and thumped it like a cantaloupe many times. Soon the mechanic went inside and came back with a jack and crawled underneath the car to look at the chassis. He spent a half hour under there, going all over the place, staying as far away from the flat tire as possible. Sobie watched him with a mixture of curiosity and amusement and aggravation. She gave me a look every once in a while as if to say: Here we are. This is what we're doing. This is our life.

When the mechanic was good and ready he stripped the lug nuts and yanked off the flat tire. The fix was some kind of gum. He put it in his mouth, chewed it, and plugged the hole with the wad. Then he pumped up the tire with his air compressor, replaced it on the axle, and suggested the bandage wouldn't last forever but it would let us finish our trip. We paid him a nominal sum and left.

Pulling back onto the highway, Sobie was smiling. "I knew it," she said. "I knew he was a genius. As soon as I saw him, I knew it."

*   *   *

We crossed the rest of the high plains by noon and started our descent to the ocean. The air gradually changed, turning from arid to thickly humid. The breeze slowed. We followed the signs to San Blas until they led us to a white dirt road going west, toward the big sky over the Pacific. The road went on for miles, unbending, through a low jungle of mango, palm, and banana trees. The smoke wasn't a problem anymore, but we still couldn't see the sun. We were inside a giant, muggy clamshell.

We weren't the only ones on the road, but it wasn't as busy as we'd expected. Most of the Totality tourists were heading to beaches with better amenities, we figured. This was still a less developed stretch of coastline, the paths rocky and potholed. For large parts of the year, the humidity was suffocating, and the whole area had historically been a breeding ground for malaria, dysentery, and typhoid. The port at San Blas had been too small to support a major city, I'd learned. The Spanish had never invested in infrastructure, and so the town's fate had been sealed.

The town was a small, drowsy place of humble shacks, organized around a minimal zocalo with a battered, concrete gazebo. There was a tienda with milk crates of spiny jungle fruits in the front, and bags of sugar and instant coffee on the half-empty shelves. The sandy streets were strewn with shells and dried grass. Even now, a day away from the Totality, the mood was torpid.

I'd made the reservations with a local agent of some kind. We went to an office thinking we needed a key, but we didn't need anything. There was no door on the hut, the agent explained. We just had to go there and start enjoying ourselves. The beach was a mile away. There was only one road.

We drove the last short leg and found our area. It was at the edge of a sheltered cove, a little indentation in the undulating coastline. Our inlet was rimmed with tan sand, fringed with palms and red mangrove. The beach was not like a postcard. The sand was lumpy, riddled with rocks and sticks and a kind of seaside mange, but to a real traveler, it was the best kind of place—pretty enough, untrammeled, private, sweet.

Our campsite was one of a handful of concrete pads planted on the edge of the sand, hidden from each other by the jungle brush. The hut was a concrete box with a thatched rooftop, a window on each wall, and a main portal. There was a metal box with hammocks rolled inside, and hammock hooks were bolted into the exterior walls and nearby palm trees. We didn't see anyone else, but we could hear a child somewhere, which meant we weren't wholly alone. If the wind kept the mosquitos from settling, it was all we'd need.

We carried our packs from the car and stripped immediately and put on our swimming suits. Sobie had been waiting for this moment. She slicked on some sunscreen and donned a straw hat she'd somehow secreted in her bag. We hurried across the spit of dirty beach, digging our feet in the hot sand, and after choosing our patch and stashing our towels and bags, went directly to the water, which we found was almost undetectable to the touch, the temperature of blood.

Sobie pushed into the rounding waves and plunged all the way in. She came up with her face to the sun, her eyes closed.

"Ahh, yes!"

She turned and threw herself into the waves again, and again rose from the water, streaming and smiling.

"I'm never leaving," she said. "This is where you can find me."

I dove into the waves a few times and swam out to the gentle breakers, feeling my muscles stretching, driving me through the warm water. I swam in a wide arc, my ears ringing, and came back to the beach, where I let the waves hit my chest and bash me onto the ocean floor. The waves surged and broke on top of me. I went under in roaring chaos and came up into the sun dizzy.

I took a break on the sand and watched Sobie playing in the surf. Her body appeared and disappeared, turning away, diving again, as the waves sizzled and dissolved. The sun needled me everywhere. My rash looked fine in the open light, and the rawness in my throat was impossible to detect. I pushed sand over my legs, letting the particles trickle over my skin. Soon Sobie returned to let herself dry in the air. Her shadow morphed on the ground near my legs, binding us.

"Hungry?" she said.

"Not yet," I said.

"God, I love not being cold," she said, and ran back to the waves.

Midway through the afternoon we put on some clothes and walked into town to shop for food. We kept our eyes out for alligators, but we only saw plovers, parrots, and Aztec rails flying in the lemon and cedar trees. At the store we bought avocados, white cheddar cheese, sourdough rolls, potato chips, and a coconut, and by the time we got back to our hut, we were famished. Already our belongings were scattered everywhere, mostly because of Sobie. She used every surface, every knob, claiming ownership of everything. In the middle of the room, she crouched on the floor and opened the bread with her fingers. She halved the avocados, sliced hunks of cheese, and made us quick sandwiches on the concrete, while I took the coconut and hammered at it on the windowsill. I managed to bash a hole in the skin, and we drank the water straight from the hairy skull. Then I bashed the globe to pieces and we ate the meat.

After lunch, we took a walk, going rock to rock and shell to shell, finding ropes of kelp, a broken jellyfish, a fragment of glass. We spotted some sea turtles walking into the wild reeds. Soon we found ourselves alone on a long, empty beach. We walked farther and started playing the game of last people on earth, which wasn't much different from first people on earth. We were bipedal humanoids, using our hands to grasp and our eyes to scan. We didn't know anything about the world beyond our sight lines. We worshipped no gods. The game eventually devolved into taking off our clothes and having furtive sex in a half-sheltered cove.

Afterward, we headed back to our area and ate potato chips, Sobie's favorite. We lay on the beach and watched the clouds filling the sky again, drawing over us like a warm blanket stitched with purple shadows. We talked mostly about Cave and the coming confrontation, which Sobie had been hearing about glancingly for weeks but which we'd never discussed in explicit detail. We talked quietly, openly, pausing often, coming at the situation from different angles. I told her about Aliyah's great competence, Liu's generous enthusiasm, Cave's seeming genuine affection. She was curious, but also skeptical in some way. She seemed to find something in the story that was hard to grasp, it was so far outside her normal life.

"It must be weird," she said, her eyes on the horizon, "doing what you do."

"What do you mean?" I said. I was watching the horizon, too. The color at the line of water and sky was turning a rare tangerine.

"I mean meeting people and lying to them like that," she said. "Using them that way. I don't mean to sound harsh or anything, but that's kind of what it is, isn't it? Selling people out?"

"It is," I said. "That's true. But that's the cost of having newspapers in the world, isn't it? If people want to know what's happening, someone has to go find out and publish it in public."

The waves whispered, and whispered again. A little crab struggled in the sand. Sobie was still seeking some kind of deeper understanding.

"I guess it isn't much of a story unless you expose something people don't want you to know," she said.

"That's true," I said.

"Cave will probably go to jail for this, though, won't he?" she said.

"Definitely," I said.

"And you like him," she said.

"I do," I said.

"And that doesn't bother you?" she said.

"It doesn't change what he did," I said.

The waves sighed. Sobie still seemed to be trying to put all these pieces together.

"How does it help anything?" she said. "That's my question. It isn't going to bring back the Indian leopard. It isn't going to bring back the whooping crane. He's living his little life in Guadalajara. He isn't hurting anyone right now. He doesn't have any power. Why do it?"

"It isn't only about him," I said. "It's about other people, too. It's about setting an example."

"I hear some moms say things like that," she said. "The death penalty argument. I don't know if I buy it."

"Actions have to have consequences," I said. "It's the only way to get some people to behave. That's what the Trials told us, didn't they? Someone is actually responsible."

"I suppose," she said. "You don't think it's just a way to make everyone else in the world feel innocent?"

We let the subject drop. We seemed to understand we'd found a difference of opinion between us, a difference of perception, and there was no need to explore any further. She'd glimpsed something rigid in me, something self-justifying. I'd seen something wishful and naive in her. We both seemed to file the observations away for some later accounting, hoping we'd never have to return to them at all.

The sun set. We strung the hammocks outside. We made more sandwiches for dinner and brushed our teeth with bottled water. We went to bed.

At night, animals came. At first I wasn't sure what was happening or what the visitors were. I was half-asleep, and they were like living shadows creeping underneath us, three or a dozen, I couldn't tell. They wandered through the camp, snuffling under the hammocks, seeking scraps of food, rooting in the beach grass. It was only when I felt the coarse hair on one of their muscled backs that I understood they were pigs. The herd loitered in our site for a few minutes and moved on, to the next hut, or into the sea, I had no idea.

* * *

In the morning, a rooster called us awake. We made coffee using the car's electricity and the water we'd brought from the city and swam under the faint white ceiling of the sky. Midmorning, we went to town and found pastries and a bag of mangoes and more chips, spotting a few Totality seekers but not nearly the crowds we'd been expecting. It was becoming obvious the coast of Mexico was enormous.

When we got back to our area, there were a few new visitors on our beach. They showed up with their towels and coolers and wandered to free patches of sand, staking their ground. There was plenty of room for everybody, even as they continued coming throughout the morning. They came mostly in small groups—Mexican families, North American families, a few German speakers, one couple we heard say they were from Ghana.

The mood was festive but hushed. Around lunchtime, a young Mexican boy appeared and started going from group to group, selling beaded necklaces from a heavy tangle around his wrist. He looked about ten years old, with bandy legs and a curved, naked belly. He never paused and never rested. He wasn't pushy, but nor was he bashful. I admired his work ethic. When he finally got to us, he displayed his wares without any special enthusiasm. He seemed resigned to our gringo miserliness but also not surprised when Sobie asked to look at the goods more closely.

"Buen precio, para usted," he said.

The necklaces were colorful agglomerations of tiny beads and death heads. Coral, emerald, amethyst, in dense, random combinations. Sobie pulled one from the boy's hands and put it around her neck, the beads clattering softly, the colors flashing.

"Looks good on you," I said.

"You think?" she said.

"I do," I said.

"What looks good down here doesn't always look good up in the States," she said, reaching into her bag for a few pesos. "We'll see if it's a keeper when I get back."

By early afternoon, the pale moon had emerged over the horizon, climbing toward the sun's trajectory. The collision course was already clear. The game of celestial, slow-motion chicken had begun.

We spent part of the wait learning about the eclipse on our phones. The word *eclipse* came from the Greek "disappearance," or "abandonment," we found. For the Aztecs, an eclipse meant the death of the sun god Tonatiuh at the hands of a monster and brought fear that children would be born without lips or noses, or cross-eyed, or as mice. The Incas believed an eclipse foretold the death of a prince and sacrificed young boys, girls, and livestock. The ancient Chinese believed a celestial dragon devoured the sun. Interestingly, the ancient Egyptians left no record of solar eclipses at all.

As the time narrowed, we started putting on our polarized glasses every few minutes to check the progress and get used to the sun's dim circle in the plastic field. We laid out our towels and opened a new pack of chips, knowing we wouldn't move again. All around us, the audience was becoming more charged, more focused. The animals in the jungle seemed to become quiet. Even the breeze stilled. The whole world seemed to understand that distant, powerful forces were at work, drawing its attention to the sky.

In the ocean, a few swimmers wearing glasses floated faceup, watching the blue screen over their heads. On the wet sand, a few children built a castle, no idea what was happening in the sky above them. We started checking the moon's and sun's positions with our glasses every few seconds as the distance closed.

We watched as the pale, bald orb of the moon edged closer and closer. The bright, shaggy orb of the sun seemed to wait. Almost tentatively, the two orbs seemed to lean toward each other, seeking the proper angle.

At last, the sun and moon touched.

Immediately, the light of the whole galaxy changed. Moon-shaped shadows fell under the trees, becoming a mess of overlapping crescents, and faded to darkness as the moon sank deeper into the sun's body. As the edges of the spheres merged, like two beads of water joining, the whole sky shifted from blue to a nauseous, yellowish green. Black light seemed to emanate from the ocean. Muted iridescence tingled on the surfaces of the plants. The trees became rimmed in dark outlines, glowing inside gray aureoles.

The moon continued pushing into the sun's fire, cutting the sun into a quarter, a half. Finally, the moon completely covered the solar disc. The edges sealed perfectly, and the moon's shadow, the umbra, fell over the world. For a long moment, our globe, the moon's globe, and the sun's globe were all in perfect alignment, like a straight billiard shot. We were in the swirl of a shell, the whorl of a tornado, observers in a vast, incomprehensible machine. We were pilots in the cockpit of a planetary fighter jet, streaming over the edge of time. Sobie glanced at me, and we shared a wild look before we both started laughing and turned back to the sky.

And as quickly as the eclipse started, it began to end. The halo of the corona was already bubbling on the edges of the black disc and a flare of diamond appeared on the outer ring. The moon and sun parted, beads of fire appearing on the lip of the bond. The edging grew into a sliver of fire, and the crack widened, letting the heat and light back down to the earth. Light showered across the surface of the ocean, returning all the dazzling color. The jungle's breath returned; sound returned. The dark scintillation rose up into everyday brightness.

The crowd on the beach began applauding. The children were already romping again, only half-aware of what they'd just witnessed. "Again, again," someone yelled. Others echoed the call. Everyone seemed to agree they hadn't known what to expect. Only that, like us, they hadn't been ready.

It was a few hours later that my fever came on.

13

The first chills started in the afternoon—little, placeless tremors that I tried to ignore, hoping they might be light breezes moving in the wrong direction or some extended itch from my rash. I tried putting them out of my mind, but by late afternoon my strength was fading. By dinner I couldn't pretend that the sickness wasn't real. Every surface of my body chafed. I had no appetite. I kept the news from Sobie, not wanting to worry her. But at a certain point, I could no longer keep it from myself.

Sobie went to sleep early, worn out by the days of swimming and sun. Her flight home was in the afternoon, which meant we had to leave the beach first thing in the morning. I tried to sleep, but the fever wouldn't let me, sending small charges over my skin, one spot and then another. My stomach wasn't right, either. Faucets had opened, and fluids were burbling down into my lower intestines. Every few minutes, I had to crawl silently into the brush and drain myself. I felt better for a minute and came back, and soon the rumble started again. I rose, plodded to a new place, squatted, barely noticing the putrid stink for all my panting.

It went on all night. As the sun rose, I finally got up and sat on the sand, staring at the gray water. When Sobie woke up she quietly approached me. The stars were still out. She touched my shoulders, but the tenderness quickly became concern.

"Are you okay?" she said. "You're burning up."

"I'm okay," I said, but I found I couldn't turn around and look at her. My teeth were chattering. My skin was covered in shifting patches of goose bumps.

"You're sure?" she said.

"It was probably something I ate," I said.

"We ate all the same things, didn't we?" she said.

"Or drank, I don't know."

The sun rose higher and the sky filled with color. Sobie made herself coffee and packed the car while I sat in a patch of shade. I wanted to help her, but I couldn't manage to stand up. I could only listen to her throwing her things into her bag, tossing her bag into the trunk. Sometimes I turned and watched her, but I had trouble concentrating. It seemed impossible that she could be out there, moving so easily, and I was stuck in this electrified pit.

We'd scheduled plenty of time to drive to the airport, but with only one of us functioning, the time became short. Sobie had to hurry to get the car packed and the campsite cleaned.

Into the box went the hammocks. Into the bags went the garbage. Into the trash cans went the bags. The back seat was still a shambles when we had to go.

Sobie drove. She tilted the mirror, adjusted the seat, and, without ceremony, guided us out of our inlet, bumping us along the dirt road and out of the estuary. The brackish heat billowed from the marshes, bringing the smell of fetid water, rotting fruit, and minerals. A lurid parrot, flushed from a tree, almost hit the windshield, squawking its hate.

Two turns and we were back on the highway. One more turn and we were on the straightaway leading to the city. We climbed back up the incline, into the desert, into the sky.

The plains scrolled in reverse. The smoke was gone, and the sky was gigantic. The expanse of useless land on either side vibrated behind the glass.

We didn't talk. I couldn't hold up a conversation, anyway, and Sobie seemed too worried to entertain me. She was busy balancing her many obligations, weighing her many duties. She had duties to herself, in the form of work, house, and friends back home. She had duties to her daughter, which usurped everything. And she possibly had duties to this new person in her life who'd suddenly become an unexpected burden. She wanted to help me, I knew, but in reality she didn't have the time. She had only finite energies. We both understood that she had to go home.

The chills were running through me in powerful waves. I'd already drained myself a dozen times, but I still had to climb out every half hour to wring myself out more. I hobbled into the brush, squatted, and crawled back, not even ashamed. Every time, she handed me a thermos of water and told me to drink. I sipped the metallic water and rolled my forehead back to the cool glass, staring at the endless plains, the clouds flowing over the horizon. I was scanning for comfortable places to lie down and die out there, a sunny patch of boulders or a distant copse of saguaro. I wanted to do it under a tree or in a ditch, unwatched by anybody, no doctors or even loved ones gathered around my sweat-soaked bed. I just wanted to go off like an animal and do it in peace.

At some point, a message appeared on my phone from Cave.

"Hope the trip's going well," it read. "It looks like a good fight for us tomorrow."

The bullfight, I thought. What a concept. I'd been thinking about our meeting on and off during the trip, but now the thought became abrasive and abstract. I couldn't imagine confronting Cave in my current state. But what choice did I have? I managed to send back a thumbs-up hologram, buying time, and turned back to the window.

Moments later, another message came, this one from Aliyah. The cameraman was on the way, she wrote. His flight was leaving, and he'd be in Guadalajara by sundown. He'd come find me at the hotel when he landed. I sent her a thumbs-up, too, and turned off the sound on my phone. So the world hadn't paused. The wheels were still rolling toward me.

We passed the town with the diner and the garage. It seemed like the memory of a dream. Had we really spent a night there? Had I really met those people? I was passing myself in the far reaches of the universe. I might have spent years of my life in that town for all I knew. I might still be there now.

Eventually, the city began drawing us in. The electrical lines sped alongside us, leading us down into the basin. Sobie, with the help of the dashboard, piloted us through the traffic, hitting all the right on- and off-ramps, stealing glances at me when she could. She wore her sunglasses like a mask, but I could see the worry in her features. The calculations were already done, the choice was made. She couldn't help me, but the stress and guilt remained. She hated to leave a wounded animal like me behind, but what could she do?

"I should take you to the hospital or something," she said.

"It's okay," I said. "Just go to the airport and go home."

"But who's going to look out for you?" she said.

"I'm fine," I said. "It's just food poisoning. It's probably a twenty-four-hour thing."

She didn't argue. We were already arriving at the airport, where the crowds of Totality tourists were streaming in. They were climbing out of cars and buses, checking their bags, hugging, all embarking on their journeys back to their distant lives. I had trouble tracking anything in the bustle, confused by the muffled announcements dropping from the intercoms in slow-motion Spanish, the doors crunching closed, the luggage rumbling. I tried to help Sobie with her bags, but by the time I climbed out of the car she was already done.

"I don't know what to do," she said. "You can't drive anywhere like this."

"I can," I said. "I'm fine. Just go."

"But . . . ," she said.

"Really," I said. "Go."

The traffic was already pushing us along. We had no time to loiter. We kissed once, and she said she'd see me soon, in a matter of days. I told her I'd call her before then. She kissed me one more time, tenderly, lingeringly, and pressed her hand to my cheek. Then, suddenly, she was gone.

I returned to the car and somehow drove myself to the hotel. The air-conditioning was frigid, but I couldn't bother to change the settings. Horns were honking. Colors were smearing on the windshield. Sobie had programmed the directions, and I did exactly what the voice told me. On the way, Aliyah texted again to tell me the cameraman would be heading to the hotel when he landed. I found a parking spot on a buckled side street and fumbled in the back seat until I managed to retrieve a single flip-flop and a bottle of sunscreen.

In the hotel, the elevator was excruciatingly slow. I could hear the gears straining to move the box upward, laboring somewhere deep underground. The wracking vibrations ran up the metal cords. At last, the elevator rattled to a stop and I stumbled down the scented hallway. I unlocked the door with my card and made it into the room. I slid into the cold sheets with my clothes on.

I lay there wrapped in the sheets, quaking. The quakes became convulsions, and then, briefly, a plateau of peace, followed by more shivering and quaking. I could feel the fever grinding through me. The tremors started up again, in my shoulders, down my spine. Somewhere my phone was vibrating. I couldn't find it in time to answer, but when I dug it from my bag, I saw I'd missed a call from Aliyah. The cameraman was in the hotel now, she said. He'd be coming to meet me when he'd showered and made a few calls. Her voice seemed echoey and unreal. She said she hoped all was well.

"If there's a problem, just let me know, okay?" And even through my illness I could hear the concern, not just for me but for our whole project, for herself.

I tried to sleep for a while, but the fever kept shocking me awake. I wasn't sure how I'd be able to talk to the cameraman when he appeared. The thought of him returned again and again in my mind but never resolved. If I could conserve my energy, I hoped, maybe I could muster a burst of strength for the meeting. And then another burst in the morning for the Donaldson. It seemed impossible, but I had to try. I tried to lie as still as possible, but the fever kept rubbing me, I squirmed on the mattress, trying to escape, but every path was blocked. The sheets tangled around me as I writhed, half-sleeping, trying to shed my aching skin.

Soon, or maybe years later, the knock came. The cameraman was out in the hall, which meant I had to get up and let him in. I managed to stand, and the room seemed to tilt. The windows were filled with a dusky light, and beyond the rooftops, a final aquamarine stripe on the horizon. The room was too dim so I turned on an overhead light, but that was a mistake. The light attacked me. I was bombarded by streaming particles. They pierced me like X-rays. When my eyes finally got used to the brightness, I could see the room was in bad shape. My suitcase was open, and my clothes were piled on the chairs. The air smelled like rancid milk. I drank a quick bottle of water, feeling the coldness trickle through my organs, and stood there panting as the knock came again.

"Coming," I croaked.

The trip across the room was an arduous journey. I felt cold air swirling around my neck. Flecks of ice seemed to spatter against my arms and legs. The short hallway running past the bathroom was like a gloomy cave, filing to a narrow line of light at the bottom of the door where the cameraman's feet waited. At last I turned the cold handle and opened the door a crack.

"Howdy," the cameraman said. "Jack?"

"That's me," I said.

"I'm TD," he said. "It's good to meet you. I've heard great things."

The cameraman was younger than I'd expected. He was somewhere in his midthirties, I thought, in that indeterminate zone that wasn't youth and wasn't middle age. His hair was sandy blond under a blue baseball cap. His face was slightly bloated and reddish. He stood there with a friendly half-grin on his lips and lidded, semi-amused eyes, waiting for me to say something, but I wasn't sure what.

"Likewise," I managed.

"Is this a good time to talk?" TD said. He could already see that I was somehow compromised. My rheumy eyes and rotten breath were giving me away.

"Yeah," I said. "I'm feeling a little sick is all. It must be something I ate. But now is good. Yes."

"In your room?" he said. "Or we could meet downstairs in the bar if that's better. Whatever you want."

"Here's fine," I said, and turned and let TD into my room.

He crossed the threshold and entered the bedroom, looking for a place to sit. He was too polite to choose a spot by himself, and I told him to go ahead and use the chair at the desk. I took the bed, still warm from my heat.

"It's really incredible what you've done down here, man," TD said, taking off his ball cap and putting it on his knee. "Aliyah was telling me all about it. I don't know how you got so deep with this guy so fast. I've been on jobs where it takes months just to make contact. But you. Whew. Way to go, man."

"I got lucky," I said, breathing heavily from the round trip to the door. "We were reading books by the same author."

"That's what Aliyah said," he said. "I've never heard of that before."

"You've worked a lot of these jobs, Aliyah told me," I said.

"I guess so," he said. "I keep busy. They keep calling me. You never want to say no. You don't know if they'll ever call again, right?"

I nodded, already exhausted. Thankfully, TD proceeded to tell me a story. The story went on for a long time, involving foreign names and places, and from the beginning I had trouble following. I blamed the fever at first, but gradually I began to realize that TD was possibly a disorganized storyteller. He seemed to loop back and repeat himself often and referred to things I couldn't possibly understand. Soon I stopped listening at all and just concentrated on his voice. His voice was soft, almost apologetic. I thought I heard a faint Southern drawl in there. Or maybe he'd been drinking, it was hard to tell. His voice went on and on, coming at me in waves. "You just never know how a thing's gonna go" was the main gist, I gathered.

Through the gentle pulsations of his voice, I tried to concentrate on his face. I looked at his mouth, his eyes, but I couldn't focus very well. The more he talked, the more his face seemed to shine in the overhead light, until it started to seem almost translucent. The top layer of skin seemed to dissolve, and the underlying skeletal structure started showing through. The lighting in the room was very bad, I thought. It was carving shadows into his face, making him look like a skull. I could see the black sockets behind his eyes, the cavities of his cheeks. I wanted to turn off the light and switch to the lamp on the desk, but I didn't want to get up, either. I had to accept the brightness even though it was peeling off our flesh.

At some point, something in his tone changed. He started sounding more practical, more logistical, and I forced myself to pay closer attention.

"So I drove past the museum on the way into town," TD said. "I took a look inside. I think that's the place for the interview. I hope we're still thinking about doing it there."

"Absolutely," I said.

"And you still have his car?" he said. "Is that right?"

"The car?" I said. "Yeah. I do have his car."

"Do we have to take it back to his house beforehand?" he said. "For you to return it, I mean?"

"Oh. I don't know," I said. "I don't think I have to return it there, no."

Why we were talking about the car, I couldn't understand. The subject of the car drop-off didn't seem important to me. If we both wanted to meet Cave at the museum, there was nothing stopping us from doing that. I had trouble remembering how we'd gotten here, but TD continued.

"If we do the interview at the house," he said, "Cave can get away from us too easily. He can just close the door on us and then we're left standing there holding our dicks. If we aren't really asking him any questions, that could be okay. But if you're planning on asking him a few questions, we should do it at the museum. You have questions, is that right?"

"I do," I said.

"So we should meet him at the museum," he said.

"I agree," I said.

"Does he know you're meeting him there?" he said.

"We agreed," I said. "Ten a.m. At the museum café."

"Okay, great," he said. "I didn't know that was already on the books. Sorry."

From the false topics of the car and the meeting place, we finally got into the actual logistics of the confrontation itself. We should arrive at the museum an hour early, TD said. We didn't need to be especially discreet when we got there. In fact, when the time came, in this kind of situation, we wanted to be extremely obvious. The subject, Cave, had to understand very clearly what was going on. The time for secrecy was over. Cave needed to understand the camera was recording him, both legally and for the dramatic value. That was why the camera he'd brought was quite large. TD said he had a big, old-fashioned TV camera he'd be using. When the time came, I would have to alert Cave and say his name out loud on camera. I should say his name on camera more than once, if possible. Maybe I could brandish a picture or document. TD had an envelope from Aliyah that contained all the proof of Cave's ID. He handed it over and said I should bring the documents in the morning and present them to Cave on camera.

"He might want you to show them to him," TD said. "He might not. You never know. Something will go wrong, I can

guarantee that, but you never know what it'll be. You try to be prepared for anything, but you have to let it all go in the moment."

"I understand," I said.

"I was down in Brazil last year," he said. "I was down there shooting a whistleblower with some financial information about the junta in charge. The only safe space we could find to talk was the middle of the Amazon River. We agreed we'd meet out there in the middle of the night in canoes. Seemed really smart. Who'd find us in the middle of the river? But turns out, controlling a canoe is not that easy. It's like paddling a tree trunk. Those Indian guys make it look easy, but it is definitely not easy, believe me. Me and the reporter guy made it to the middle of the river, but we couldn't link up with the other canoe. Our canoe kept drifting downstream and spinning in circles. We finally had to paddle back to the bank and do the interview on the shoreline. We were in the middle of doing it when the cops showed up and arrested our guy. He's still in prison. Really crazy, man. All of which is just to say, you never know."

As TD talked, his face was turning into a skull again. His eyes were flickering in and out, and his teeth were exposed under his moving lips. It was like one of those jeweled Day of the Dead faces. His skull had a festive quality. The skull told me we would take two vehicles in the morning. He'd bring his gear in his rental van, and I'd take Cave's car. Once we had Cave in our frame, we'd follow him as far as he took us.

TD rose. He seemed to understand I'd come to the end of my strength. His shifting skull face managed a look of sympathy in my direction, and he put on his hat, pausing on the way to the door.

"Anything you need," he said, "just call me. I'm here for you and your story."

"Thank you," I said.

And then TD was gone. He must have let himself out.

*   *   *

The windows were dark. I got back into bed but couldn't sleep. I tried watching TV, but the images physically hurt my eyes, like metal dragged against my corneas. I flipped through many channels, finding growling car races, dayglow cartoons, babbling talking heads. When I bumped into the pay-per-view blank screens in the high channels I cycled back down again, seeking comfort.

Finally I found a station I could tolerate. It showed a woman playing a recorder. She was performing Bach on an outdoor stage at a classical music festival in the Yucatán. It was nighttime, and the air around her seemed fragrant and warm. The stage was a wooden shell filled with rich, tobacco-colored shadows. The young musician was a person of complete elegance and beauty. Her skin was olive, and she wore a clean peasant blouse that fell perfectly across her fine shoulders and neckline.

Her hair was parted in the middle, and she never wavered, never lost her flow.

I fell in and out of sleep, listening to the woman play Bach. The sheets were like sandpaper, and although I couldn't get all the way down into unconsciousness, I had dreams, or something like dreams. I could barely think, but I understood I was on the verge of something monumental. I was about to destroy another person's life. He was someone who'd destroyed much life on the planet himself, and yet I wanted to warn him, to tell him to flee. I could still secretly inform him about what the morning would bring if I wanted to. And if he wanted to, he could still run into the night, across moonlit rivers, and hide in misty swamps. He could float on a raft down a river to freedom. I could call him even now. No one would ever know what I'd done. But I couldn't seem to move. There was a magnet in my bed sucking on the iron in my blood.

I must have fallen asleep because my dreams became deeper, more twisted. I dreamed I had an obsidian knife, and June beetle plugs in my earlobes. I dreamed amber rings in my nose, quetzal feathers with bells in my tangled hair. I dreamed incense rising into the dawn, folding, curling, becoming the coiled body of the winged serpent, Quetzalcoatl.

14

My fever broke around 3:00 a.m. I could almost feel it crack inside me and start sloughing away, like an iceberg calving into the warm sea. One minute I was writhing underneath it and the next it was gone. I was free.

I got up and went to the window and looked at the darkened city. I could see a plane descending through the low clouds, illuminating the torn mist with its landing-gear lights. I found it almost unbelievable the world could appear in such a clear, calm light. I'd had food poisoning after all, I thought. Whatever had happened was now over.

I showered, relishing the hot needles of water and billowing steam, and cleared grains of sand from my scalp with my fingernails, watching it all swirl down the drain. I put on clean clothes, the first in days, and drank four bottles of water. I texted Sobie at sunrise and told her I was feeling better. She wrote back immediately: "Good!"

I went down to the street and cleaned out the green seed, pulling the packs and sleeping bags from the trunk and throwing away the wrappers and used bottles littering the floor. I couldn't get all the sand out of the seats' creases, but I did my best. It wasn't the moment for a thorough detailing. The owner would never be driving this car again.

At the appointed hour, I drove to the museum through the quiet Sunday streets. The shops were mostly closed. The streets were damp. I parked around the block from the museum, out of view, not that that was necessary. I wasn't sure if the meters ran on Sundays, but I paid anyway, wanting to get rid of some of my Mexican coinage.

I walked into the café a few minutes after opening to find TD already there, setting up. His gear was scattered on the long table at the center of the room, and he was sorting through his many nylon pouches, beginning the process of assembling his apparatus.

"Morning, buddy," he said. "Feeling okay?"

"Better," I said.

"Far-out," he said. "You seemed pretty fried last night. I was a little worried you'd be able to make it."

"It must've been some kind of bug," I said. "Something I ate."

"That'll happen," he said.

TD went back to work, and I went to order coffee but realized when I arrived at the counter that I didn't want any after all. The thought of coffee entering my system sounded vile. I ordered herbal tea, which caused the barista to raise an eyebrow, and I left her a huge tip, knowing we'd probably never see each other again after today.

I sat near the window and watched TD. I was always amazed how long it took a cameraman to set up. He had to test all his lenses, even the lenses he wouldn't be using, and then he had to test an entire magazine of sodium-ion batteries, slotting each wafer into a portable clip and taking a reading of the illuminated spectrum. Then he had to walk around the room with a light meter, checking the levels near the windows and at the center of the room, confirming what he already knew. Then he dialed the new settings into the central digital command on his wrist.

Lastly, he withdrew his handheld microphone and brought it over to me.

"It's mostly just for show," he said. "There's a filament in there that does all the sound collecting. But the viewers like a stick with a spongey head in these kinds of situations. It helps them understand what's happening."

"Test, test, test," I said.

"Good," he said, and bent over his control pad, adjusting the levels. "Let's try getting you over near that pillar there, okay? Under that poster."

I moved over to where he was pointing and said "test" again.

"Good," TD said. "That's a good spot, if you could get him there. You'll be backlit if you stay by that window. But I can work with anything. I'll be right with you the whole time, buddy. Hopefully you'll forget I'm even here."

"I doubt I'll be forgetting anything," I said.

"Nervous is natural," he said. "It'd be weird if you weren't. I wouldn't worry, though. He doesn't seem like the violent type. A lot of the guys I've shot, they're actually pretty cool guys. Some of the worst people in the world turn out to be really nice guys. I shot a yakuza guy in Macao a few months ago, he was a sweetheart. Just wanted to play with his cat. If you're not on the wrong side of them, they're fine, for the most part."

"We'll be on the wrong side soon," I said.

"Sides change all the time," TD said, spraying a lens with a canister of compressed air. "I remember a kid I used to play basketball against. I hated that kid's guts. Fucking hated him. What a crybaby. And a cheater. Then he moved across town and joined our team. I loved him then. Fucking loved him. He's one of my best friends now. Funny how the mind works."

"I doubt your friend destroyed entire ecologies," I said.

"Probably not," TD said. "He might have, though. I wouldn't put it past him. I can't really defend him. He's kind of a terrible human. But goddamn, he's funny. The way I see it, I'm not trying to judge anybody. I'm only here to get it on film. Let the bureaucrats do the judging."

TD returned to his prep work and I went to the window to watch for Cave. I tried to clear my mind of all expectations and concerns. The plaza was empty except for a mob of pigeons and a few magpies in the trees. The morning sun seemed to stick to a patch of wet flagstones. In one distant storefront window I could make out the reflection of a man doing something, maybe talking on a phone. Soon the man disappeared from the frame and the window reflected only a red postbox.

TD went to his car and came back with his camera, which was as gigantic as promised—a cannon-size barrel fitted to a beefy, squared-off body, with a wide-screen viewfinder rising off the back. It looked like an antique TV camera from the 1960s, it was so big, and yet because it was actually a mirrorless, hybrid model from 2045, he explained, built into a casing of woven polymer plastic, it weighed almost nothing.

TD strapped on a special vest with many dangling pouches and hooks for his tools and sound gadgets. He tightened a thick belt around his waist and carefully attached a gimbal that allowed the camera to float out in front of his chest, swiveling easily on a stabilized mount. Finally, he inserted the feather-weight camera itself with its narrow handlebars, turning himself into a kind of centaur. As the final minutes ticked away, he did some breathing exercises and deep knee bends, and all the while the barista watched us with mild curiosity from her counter, pretending to dry a cup.

*   *   *

Cave appeared at three minutes after 10:00 a.m. He entered the square on the far side, strolling in at a leisurely pace. He had on a sharp fedora and a forest green wool hunting coat, like an English gentleman on a morning pheasant hunt. Over his shoulder he carried his leather knapsack and around his neck a pair of antique binoculars, two big, silly-looking cylinders rimmed in gold. He might even have been whistling to himself.

I kept my mind empty. I didn't think about his outfit. I didn't think about the consequences of his punishment or whether the punishment was ultimately just. I didn't worry about everyone's need to believe themselves clean and pure. I didn't even think about the ruined rain forests, or poisoned aquifers, or dead copper mines. I simply watched Cave strolling across the plaza, enjoying the pale winter sun, coming closer and closer by the moment. Even now, at this late juncture, I wasn't sure what I hoped would happen. I welcomed anyone else to come in and decide.

Soon Cave disappeared into the entrance, and TD and I took our places in the café. TD stood near the door, so as to block the way out. I sat in my usual spot, at my table, to coax Cave deeper into the room. The barista stood in her usual place, too, looking perplexed.

Moments later, Cave's shuffling steps sounded in the breezeway. His shadow fell on the doorjamb. At last, he entered, as cheerful as always.

"Morning, Jake," he said, doffing his hat. "Just let me get my coffee and then we can get going, all right?"

"Take your time," I said.

"You want anything?" he said.

"I'm okay," I said.

"The weather was good on the beach, I hope?" he said. "You had a good time?"

"Weather was fine," I said. "It was very nice."

"We didn't see much of the eclipse here," he said. "They say we were too far south. Ah well. Too bad for us."

Cave had almost reached the barista's station when he noticed TD and the giant camera trained on him. His gait slowed, and his expression clouded. He turned toward me as if to ask a question and noticed I was holding the old-fashioned microphone. Already, without a word, he was understanding the new arrangement in the room.

"What's going on here, Jake?" he said.

"I'm a reporter, Bob," I said. "I work for a news organization in the United States called the *Constant Globe*. I came here to find you and hopefully talk to you. We know who you are."

"Oh?" he said. "And who is that?"

"You're Robert Cave," I said. "Former vice president at NovaChem, tried and convicted in Toronto in 2032 for crimes against life. You've been living in hiding in Guadalajara for almost twenty years. Is that correct?"

"I'm not sure that it is," he said.

"We've been collecting facial metrics and vocal signatures," I said, showing him my folder. "We have all the data to confirm your identity. Well beyond the legal threshold."

The evolution of Cave's understanding of what was happening took another few seconds to complete. His expression of friendly greeting faded, and notes of disappointment and hurt entered his features. A minuscule flicker of anger registered, a flash of regret, or maybe disbelief. Then he seemed to go inside himself for a moment and tabulate something in his mind, teasing out the ramifications of what he was seeing. If we were here, that meant others were out there, too. The world had reorganized outside his view. The cage of his life was at last closing on him.

"Interesting," he said.

"A lot of people would like to hear your story," I said. "They want to know how you got here and what you've been doing all this time. If you'd like to sit down, we'd love to ask you some questions."

"Oh, that's all right," he said. "I've got nothing to say right now, Jake. I think you two guys must have the wrong idea."

"We can just sit here and talk," I said. "On the record this time."

"Oh, I don't think so," he said. "I'd rather not. You know, I still need that coffee."

Cave turned to the coffee counter and greeted the barista with a shaky bow. He asked for his regular café de olla in a paper cup, please. He didn't try to make conversation anymore, but continued to smile and look around the room while the barista made his drink. No one in the room spoke. Cave sent his gaze onto one thing and then another, as if sealing it all in his memory. He looked at the posters, the potted plants. His gaze landed on me sometimes, too. There was so much to take in. He was probably scrolling over the past weeks, revisiting all our moments together. The coincidence of the book was going to be hard to resolve.

He paid and took possession of his cup. Then he started ambling toward the door.

"Are you leaving?" I said.

"We're going to the bullfight, aren't we?" he said. "You're still coming, I assume?"

Cave navigated around TD and the camera and continued on his way. As he wandered out the door, I glanced at TD, who nodded with encouragement. This was good, he was saying. This was in fact gold. We should follow.

We trailed Cave out of the museum into the late-morning sun. The light was still fresh, and the air was fragrant with the scent of wet pavement and tea olive plants. The last moisture was starting to steam away, and it was turning into a beautiful, balmy day. Cave strolled across the shining courtyard, sipping his coffee, scaring a gang of pigeons into the air. As soon as they re-formed we scattered them again.

He walked onto Avenida República, one of the main arteries leading to the center of the city. The traffic was light, with only a few Sunday morning cars on the road and a trickle of pedestrians on the sidewalks. TD was in his element now, piloting his floating camera with smooth command. He ran ahead and walked backward for a while, as I joined Cave's side, asking him more questions.

"Are you in touch with anyone from before the Trials?" I said.
Cave didn't answer.

"Do you ever see your family?" I said. "Do you ever travel
to the States?"

No answer.

"How do you maintain a stream of income as a fugitive?" I
said. "Is your house paid for?"

Still no answers. He kept walking, staring straight ahead.
Along the way he discarded his coffee in a trash can. He didn't
seem to want it after all.

"Why don't you tell me about your trip, Jake?" he said eventually, as if noticing me for the first time. "What happened at
the beach? I'd like to hear about that."

"It was nice," I said. "The weather was good, like I said."

"And the car did all right?" he said.

"We got a flat tire, actually," I said.

"No kidding," he said. "What did you do?"

I told him about fixing the flat tire and our time at the beach,
how sick I'd gotten. None of it was usable as audio, I assumed,
but I hoped it would somehow bring him back into the conversation at hand. He seemed unfazed, unable or unwilling to
acknowledge the reality of what was happening. Maybe a friendly
digression would reel him back in.

"We saw some turtles on the beach," I said.

"Oh?" he said. "What kind?"

"I'm not sure," I said.

"Mexico has five species of sea turtle," he said. "They date back to the Mesozoic. That's at least sixty-five million years ago. Inconceivable, isn't it? They're a symbol of hope and good fortune. But only one in a thousand lives to adulthood."

"They're beautiful swimmers," I said.

"Like birds underwater," he said. "It's true."

We kept walking, talking about the beach, and the foot traffic began to get heavier. TD started to have trouble pushing through the pedestrians and had to fall back and strike a position behind us, walking in our wake. The other pedestrians barely seemed to notice us as we pressed onward. They were city people. They saw people shooting TV shows all the time. As the crowd got thicker, I couldn't keep a proper distance or speak over the din. I gave up on the questioning and fell back and joined TD.

"This is great," TD said. "We're deep in the pocket, man. Just keep going. Keep going. We'll see where this goes."

The sidewalk was becoming more congested by the block, mostly with men. Short men, tall men, fat men, and thin men, hailing mainly from the city, but from the country, too, judging by their guayaberas, the shirts with the rows of pleats on the chests. There were a fair number of tourists as well, in their UV-resistant fabrics and fanny packs. We went another two blocks, gathering fans, before the Plaza de Toros Municipal de Guadalajara appeared.

The arena was a giant concrete cylinder painted bright red and yellow, with flags flying on the topmost rim. We followed

Cave up the hill and onto the grounds, passing food carts, souvenir booths, taco stands, and tamale vendors. I saw a goat head half-stripped of flesh, fatty chunks of meat falling off the bones, and a woman scooping sacks of salted crickets into a plastic bag. I saw sugared churros, pan dulces, pistachios, and corn nuts, all manner of colors and smells beaming through the clear prism of my mind.

Cave approached the ticket booth and purchased a ticket and passed inside. We followed close behind, entering the echoey honeycomb of the arena. The tunnel was cavernous and dark and reeked of old beer. The sounds of marching feet and voices bounced all around the walls. Many of the men were already drunk, it seemed, yelling, singing, passing around their leather botas of tequila.

The hallway canted upward, drawing the trudging crowd higher. We followed Cave to the uppermost level, where he turned and jostled for the arched light of the doorway, momentarily becoming a black silhouette in the glare. We went after him and emerged into the core of the arena, a giant, sun-filled pit encircling a pad of yellow earth.

Rising in row after row were men, thousands of men. They were singing, smoking, laughing, drinking, awaiting the ritual destruction of the day's bull. Trumpets and mandolins played, but most of all, cymbals, a constant clattering from every direction. Somewhere a man cried, "Olé!"

"Aliyah texted," TD said, shoving his camera through the crowd. "If we can keep him here, that would be great. The police are on the way."

"That fast?" I said.

"Aliyah has her ways," he said. "She's always a few steps ahead. You know that, though."

We'd emerged on the shady side of the circle, the sombra, and Cave began skirting the curve of the bleachers, looking for a place to sit. The first section was already filled, so he moved along the railing to the next section, edging closer to the hard line dividing shadow and sun. The cymbals were constant, and soon more trumpets joined in, as down on the field the matadors and picadors in their gilded uniforms began entering. Some were carried on horses guided by men in white pajamas with red sashes; some entered on foot. Around the whole circle, the crowd cheered.

At last Cave found a seat, one fedora in a sea of sombreros and sports caps. TD paused on the catwalk, unable to take his giant camera any farther.

"Keep going," he said. "I can shoot from up here. The mic will pick up everything. This is a great shot. Pure dynamite."

I pressed onward, descending the steps and maneuvering into Cave's aisle. Kindly, he made space for me on the bench. On either side of us, men were yelling.

"Good crowd today," Cave said. "Some days it isn't so full. But today, this is a real crowd."

"You used to come pretty often, you said?"

"Not that often," he said. "But sometimes. I remember seeing a matador get thrown ten feet in the air one time. His shoes flew off his feet. He had to finish the fight in his stockings. That was a performance."

The horses and men continued parading around the ring, presenting themselves in loose formation. Across the stadium a row of women began waving white handkerchiefs. The smell of aftershave and cheap cigars wafted through powerfully.

"You know, it's a myth that bulls hate red," Cave said, adjusting his hat to block the sun. "They're essentially colorblind. They only see two colors, whereas we see three. They're dichromats, is what they're called."

"How did you make it to Guadalajara, anyway?" I said. "Was this your first choice as a place to hide?"

"It's the motion of the cape," he said, gesturing at the scene below, "the muleta, that gets them so riled up. Not the color."

"Did you go anywhere else before you landed here?" I asked. "Did you have to pay anyone for passage? Or identification? Were any institutions involved?"

"They're also social animals," he said, "which is a big factor. You have to imagine it from the bull's point of view. They're ripped away from their herd and thrown into the ring with all these people screaming at them. Of course they get angry. The cape waving in front of their faces is actually the least of their worries. Funny how people think it's all about the color, isn't it?"

"Do you have any idea where the other Empty Chairs are?" I said. "Have you had any contact?"

By now, the ring was beginning to clear. Only a small group of men in tasseled uniforms remained, waiting for the bull's entry. The crowd quieted. The band stopped playing. A door opened, and the bull emerged. He charged out onto the bright, dusty ground, hooves pounding, and rumbled through his new environment, exploring his new situation. The crowd applauded and whistled as the bull rounded the circle, goaded by the banderilleros with their fuchsia capes.

"They're testing his strength now," Cave said. "They're looking for any weaknesses or quirks. This looks like a pretty powerful bull, I'd say."

It was a beautiful bull. His burly, muscled shoulders tapered to a massive chest, and his rear haunches were speckled with gray spots. His horns were short and thick, the yellowish bone curving to blackened points. He lumbered from one patch of ground to another, disregarding the chalked lines, fixated on whatever man appeared in front of him.

"They'll start bleeding him now," Cave said. "Watch. This is an art form."

The picador entered the ring astride a horse in quilted armor. The horse and rider engaged the bull in a series of brisk chases, nearly getting gored numerous times but always cantering free just before the bull could touch them. Whenever possible, the picador turned in his saddle and stabbed the bull's mounded shoulder, leaving a dangling necklace of sharp, barbed sticks.

"They used to do this without armor for the horses," Cave said, "if you can believe that. More horses died during a bullfight than bulls. By far. The horse is the unsung hero of the bullfighting tradition."

At last, the matador reentered the ring, alone this time. The crowd cheered. The bull was now decorated with six colorful barbs, and blood was oozing from his neck, his tongue lolling. The matador walked slowly to the center of the circle, struck a position, and began to turn his cape, leading the dying bull through his paces. He carved short arcs in the air, holding the cape far and then close to his body. Over and over, the bull pushed forward, attacking. The crowd whistled and applauded each time.

The matador and the bull drifted from zone to zone, presenting to different sections of the audience. Cave was done explaining the fight to me. He didn't say anything about the style of the matador's gestures or the subtleties of the bull's movements. For my part, I'd given up asking questions. The only dignity now was in silence. I could allow him that much.

The bull was still alive when the police arrived. They stood at the end of the row, two men in beige uniforms, one with a mustache, the other too thin for his epaulets. The crowd barely seemed to notice their presence but collectively made a pocket of space. The police gestured sternly at Cave to come with them. He didn't respond directly, but he didn't resist. He stood up, brushed off his pants, and took one last look at the arena. His eyes didn't appear crazed or accusing, or forgiving, for that matter. He seemed calm.

"Goodbye, Jake," he said, edging down the row. "I hope you're feeling better soon."

"Goodbye, Bob," I said. I thought about saying "good luck" but refrained. It seemed like too much, given everything.

The police led Cave up the stairs, and I sat for a minute in the crowd. Sun poured down on the matador and the bull, and the cheap cigar smoke and aftershave blew through again. The crowd cheered wildly about something in the ring, but by the time I looked, I'd missed it.

*   *   *

I exited before the fight was over. The men in my row stood and made way, and the open space on the bench closed behind me. I climbed the stairs to TD and handed over the microphone.

"Nice work, buddy," he said. "Great stuff. I mean, come on, look at this place. I'm sticking around to get a little more footage, okay? I can meet you back at the hotel in an hour or so. That sound good?"

"Sounds good," I said, and kept walking.

At the top of the stairs, I turned for one more view of the ring. The bull stood immobile on the yellow ground, his shoulders and flanks black with blood. The matador stood a few paces away, his back turned, chin upraised. The crowd was roaring. And with that picture in mind, I turned and headed out.

I walked through the arched doorway, down the dank halls, through the turnstiles, into the city. In the market, the vendors were hunched over their scuffed plastic bowls, eating their lunch. On the sidewalk, a few city workers cleared the gutters with their buzzing solar leaf blowers.

My phone vibrated with texts from Aliyah. She was sending me holograms of trophies, gold medals, and shooting stars, and I texted her back the same. I'd thought she might call, but apparently she didn't think that was necessary. She was already moving on to the next chapter—cataloging the new footage, starting in on the final edit. I'd served my purpose for the time being. She had to work.

I called Sobie and caught her driving to pick up her daughter from daycare. She couldn't talk long, she said, which was just as well, because my phone was almost dead.

"So it happened?" she said.

"Yeah," I said. "It did."

"And?" she said.

"And I don't know," I said. "I'm still thinking about it."

"Did he say anything?" she said. "Did he do anything?"

"He said a lot of things," I said. "We went to the bullfight."

"Well, hurry up and get home so you can tell me all about it, all right?" she said. "Oh. Here she comes. Eileen! Over here! She doesn't see me. I've got to go, Jack. I'll talk to you later, all right? Bye."

"Bye," I said.

The moment after we hung up, I realized how incredibly tired I was. The exhaustion hit me like a wave. My limbs became heavy; my brain became thick. After all the weeks of work and anticipation, of duplicity, of sickness, my body needed to shut down completely for a while. I wanted to go back to the hotel and sleep for days.

I began walking toward the hotel, and the cheers of the arena faded behind me. I took República the same way we'd come, avoiding the churchgoers and the women with their shopping bags, and at the first roundabout took a side street that I thought might be a shortcut. I passed a cathedral with blue turrets, a grocery megastore, a flock of children on bikes. Soon, I realized I was in a neighborhood I didn't recognize. I could hear bells somewhere, but they didn't help.

The hotel had to be close, I thought. But which way was it? I would've mapped it, but my phone was fully dead now, and I was left to navigate by my own compass. I took a turn, and then another turn, and ended up at a giant city park encircled by a wrought-iron fence. I followed the fence to a gate down the block that led onto a pebble pathway. The pathway led into an arbor of trees with slender, white trunks, and from there, I assumed, all the way to the other side of the park. I entered.

The park was ablaze with tropical flowers. Strange birdsongs floated from the trees. I passed a murky-looking pond, a popcorn vendor, a treacherous-looking play structure where a few children climbed. The deeper I went, the more familiar the park seemed, but I couldn't place when I'd ever been there. Vague memories floated in my mind, eluding my grasp. Maybe I was thinking of another park, in another country.

The path eventually led to a fountain in a simple brick plaza. In an unadorned stone basin, four geysers rose and crumbled. I was too exhausted to keep walking anymore, so I sat on a bench where I could watch the water falling into the pool. The surface of the pool coursed with light and shadow. Some teenagers were skateboarding on the steps nearby. A young couple was photographing a toddler on the grass.

The sun felt good on my arms. The water droplets from the fountain gave me mild chills, but I didn't mind. I'd be home soon, I told myself.

Solidarity with water, I thought. Solidarity with wind.

By now, Sobie and her daughter were home, getting ready for dinner, I thought. I wanted to buy them both gifts before I left, but I didn't know what Eileen wanted. And how old was she again? I couldn't find the number in my mind.

Up in the sky, a single cloud was visible. The cloud was a tugboat for a minute, then a feather. I watched it for a long time, shifting in the high currents. I closed my eyes, and bright orange blood coursed on my lids. I opened my eyes, and the cloud was gone.

Solidarity with sun, I thought. The sun felt warm. Solidarity with cloud. Solidarity with blue.

Acknowledgments

My immeasurable gratitude goes to Bill Clegg, whose early enthusiasm and brilliant insights allowed this book to come into being. Thank you, Bill, and everyone at the Clegg Agency.

Equal gratitude goes to Sean Manning, whose vision and stamina deepened every paragraph. I've never experienced anything like it. Thank you, Sean, and everyone at Simon & Schuster.

Thank you also to the many readers who helped so much along the way: Emily Chenoweth, Carole Raymond, Kelly Reichardt, Todd Haynes, Mattathias Schwartz, James Yu, Rob Spillman, Tony Perez, David Karp, Anna DeRoy, and Christina Lee.

And thank you to the many readers who live in my head and offer guidance without even knowing it: Camela Raymond, TM Raymond, Kit Colman, Megan Aguilar, Anne Hogle, Storm Tharp, Julia Bryan-Wilson, Sean Byrne, Mark Hansen,

ACKNOWLEDGMENTS

Tony Zito, Sarah Xel Thompson, Domenick Ammirati, Ed Johnson, Holly Cundiff, Mike Brophy, Randy Gragg, Cynthia Lahti, Howard Rodman, James Ponsoldt, Chris Blauvelt, Neil Kopp, Anish Savjani, Lance Cleland, Cheston Knapp, Santi Holley, Michael Ray, Malia Jensen, Cynthia Star, Sara Lund, Rob Mackey, Julie Weiss, Steve Doughton, Erin Boberg Doughton, Steve Malkmus, Jessica Jackson Hutchins, Eric Isaacson, Patrick Dewitt, Libby Werbel, Brian Mumford, Josh Berger, and Chris Johanson, among many others. Thank you all.

And always, thank you, Emily Chenoweth, not as a reader and writer this time, but as a life partner without whom I don't know what my life would be. And thank you, Eliza and Josephine. I love you. Now please empty the dishwasher.